The first time she'd heard about Reed, she'd known exactly what kind of guy he was.

A playboy. A forever bachelor. A man who avoided responsibility. The kind of man she'd fallen for before, and the kind of man she knew she had to avoid at all costs. She'd gone through the roller coaster ride men like that brought with them. And she knew she risked having her heart completely shredded by such a man.

But a man who avoided responsibility wouldn't feel obligated to a baby, would he? Especially one he didn't know for certain belonged to him. That man wouldn't put his life on hold and travel across the country because he was worried.

For a man who said he wanted to avoid responsibility, in the last few hours Reed Tanner had gone out of his way to take it on his shoulders. And that realization made Josie Dawson fall even harder for both Reed Tanner and the precious baby boy.

ANN VOSS PETERSON

COVERT COOTCHIE-COOTCHIE-COO

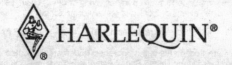

HARLEQUIN®

TORONTO • NEW YORK • LONDON
AMSTERDAM • PARIS • SYDNEY • HAMBURG
STOCKHOLM • ATHENS • TOKYO • MILAN • MADRID
PRAGUE • WARSAW • BUDAPEST • AUCKLAND

To Rita Herron
and all the fun we had working on this series.

Recycling programs
for this product may
not exist in your area.

ISBN-13: 978-0-373-69427-3

COVERT COOTCHIE-COOTCHIE-COO

Copyright © 2009 by Ann Voss Peterson

ABOUT THE AUTHOR

Ever since she was a little girl making her own books out of construction paper, Ann Voss Peterson wanted to write. So when it came time to choose a major at the University of Wisconsin, creative writing was her only choice. Of course, writing wasn't a *practical* choice—one needs to earn a living. So Ann found jobs ranging from proofreading legal transcripts to working with quarter horses to washing windows. But no matter how she earned her paycheck, she continued to write the type of stories that captured her heart and imagination—romantic suspense. Ann lives near Madison, Wisconsin, with her husband, her two young sons, her border collie and her quarter horse mare. Ann loves to hear from readers. E-mail her at ann@annvosspeterson.com or visit her Web site at www.annvosspeterson.com.

Books by Ann Voss Peterson

CAST OF CHARACTERS

Reed Tanner—He left Texas in order to live his own life. But when an old girlfriend leaves her baby on his catamaran, his future pulls him back into the past...and back to Texas.

Josie Dionne—She's willing to give up everything to be a mother. But can she risk giving her heart to a man she's sure will break it?

Honey Dawson—Honey spent her life searching for love and security. The birth of her twins made her happy, but now someone is looking to take them away.

Judge Teddy Wexler—Wealthy and powerful, the judge likes to collect trophies. Is he looking to add to his collection or protect what he has?

Portia Wexler—She loves her husband—both his money *and* his prestige—and she is not eager to share. How far will she go to keep what she's earned?

Teddy Wexler Junior—He's his father's son: ruthless, cunning, rich and a womanizer. He doesn't mind his father's affairs, but refuses to share a dime of inheritance with one of his whores or her bastard brats.

Tiffany Maylor—Her father owns a big jewelry store in Dallas. She's spoiled and likes attention. Anyone who gets in her way had better watch out.

Jimmy Bartow—Honey's friend loves her and wants her for himself. How far will he go to get her?

Neil Kinney—The peeping tom worshipped Honey and did time in jail for doing so. Has he decided to possess her and her twins once and for all?

Esme Hernandez—She has spent her life hiding a secret. Now she wants the truth to be told.

Chapter One

Bobby Crabb lined up the scope of his rifle on the rangy silhouette of a man unlocking the gate to Dock J. Coat collar turned up and knit cap pulled low, the guy was dressed for the weather.

Unlike Bobby.

No, when Bobby had gotten this job, he'd assumed all of California was sunshine and babes in bikinis. Too bad. He'd been waiting for the target less than a half hour, and he was already colder than a pawnbroker's smile.

Where was Honey Dawson?

The guy in the hat secured the gate behind him and ambled down the dock. His stride rolled, loose-hipped, more like a cowboy than a sailor. He headed toward a catamaran in the last slip.

The guy fit the part of the old boyfriend, all right. Reed Tanner. The one Bobby had guessed Honey was coming to see. But there was no sign of the bimbo.

Had he missed her?

Tanner climbed a small set of stairs leading to the boat's deck. Unlocking another gate, he let himself through and stepped aboard the sailboat. He disappeared into the cabin for a moment, then reappeared. Bobby didn't know much about boats, but he could guess Tanner was getting ready to take the craft out on the bay.

Honey had better get here soon…if she was coming at all.

Lowering the rifle, Bobby tucked it between his side and the wall of the Bay Seafood Shack and stuffed his trigger hand into the pocket of his long, thin duster. The pinkish yellow of dawn reached over the hills of the city and reflected off the concrete walls of Alcatraz, just a short distance from shore. Sailboats lined wooden docks in between, their masts stabbing into the sky. Few people stirred in the restaurants and shops lining the pier, but the place wouldn't be quiet too much longer.

Time was running out.

Maybe Honey Dawson had more than one boyfriend in San Francisco. God knew, she'd had plenty in Dallas. And all at the same time. Even Bobby was smart enough to know *that* would lead to trouble.

"Call me trouble," he muttered under his breath. Although he had to admit, he didn't feel much like trouble at the moment. Right now he just felt cold and in need of a hot cup of joe.

Sounds started to reach him from the shops and restaurants lining the pier. The jangle of keys. The murmur of voices. The shushing sound of a push broom. Sounds of the day beginning. Sounds that indicated his perch was getting risky.

Damn.

He'd hoped to end this. To pick off Honey Dawson as she walked down the pier. Erase her and get his hands on the babies before Fisherman's Wharf opened for business. Be back in the warm arms of Texas before nightfall to enjoy the client's cash. But somewhere, somehow, he'd gotten some bum information. Either she was here and gone, or that cute little maid at the hotel had lied to him. Whatever the answer, this place was fast becoming too busy for comfort.

Ready for a sail, the old boyfriend's boat started inching out of its slip. Tanner stood at the back, hands on the wheel, guiding the craft.

So much for the trap Bobby had set. Looked as if he was going to have to get back in touch with his patient side. Bide his time. Keep a close eye on the old boyfriend. Do some poking around. Wait for Honey to surface. Or maybe for a call telling him to buy a plane ticket.

In the meantime, he'd get himself a sweatshirt. Or two. And wish Honey Dawson had had the decency to hide her twins someplace warm.

THERE WAS SOMETHING WRONG with his boat.

Reed Tanner turned his head to eliminate the whoosh of the wind whistling past his ears. Above the flap of the sails as they unfurled against the gray sky, a sound halfway between a cat's mew and donkey's bray grated along his nerves like steel wool on rusted tin.

That couldn't be good.

He turned the rudder, easing his catamaran starboard, but the sound didn't change. He'd never heard anything quite like it. Not when he was out on the bay. But whatever the problem was, he was glad he didn't have the boat full of tourists, as he would come afternoon.

He was going to have to turn around.

Waves hit the front of the catamaran and sprayed

into the air. Water droplets misted his face and beaded on the band of his stocking cap. He loved sailing. Loved the cold spray and the biting wind. It made him feel alive and free. But at the moment he couldn't concentrate on any of those things. All he could do was worry.

A problem with the boat meant repair costs and canceling cruises. Even though his fledgling business had done gangbusters over the summer, he was heading into autumn now, and he didn't have a lot of cash to spare.

He cleared Alcatraz and veered hard to port, circling the island in a long arc. The city lifted bright across the water, rising up from the piers like some ancient fort, the morning sun cresting over the top. He squinted against the glare.

Now that he was moving in the direction of the wind, the sound seemed louder. More distinct. It sounded like…

He shook his head. He had to be losing his mind.

He streamed alongside the city, moving at a nice clip now. If he was lucky, he could repair whatever it was that was causing the sound and still get in a short test trip before he had to get back to the pier for his scheduled cruise.

As he approached the pier, he brought down the sails. The boat slowed, and he kicked in the engine. With the sails contained, he could hear the sound clearly now. And he didn't want to think too hard about what it was.

He threaded around the breakwater and headed for Pier 94. Sea lions already draped their huge bodies over the wooden docks, staking out prime sunbathing areas. One big bull gave a barking yell, and an encroaching youngster splashed into the water.

He guided the catamaran into its slip and tied it off.

Shrugging his coat tight around his shoulders, he descended the steps into the boat's cabin.

The sound was clear now and unmistakable. He followed the braying into the kitchenette. Tucked into the corner next to the refrigerator he spotted a little bucket-shaped seat, and inside…

Reed's breath caught, thick in his throat. It was a baby, all right. In his boat. It didn't make sense. It couldn't make sense.

A blue blanket snuggled around the infant, almost completely covering the little face. Words embroidered the fleece under the baby's chin. *Cootchie-Cootchie-Coo, Troy.*

Reed's mind stuttered. And he knew only one woman who would wrap her child in a blanket suffering from that extreme level of cuteness…a woman who happened to be a big Dallas Cowboys fan, a woman who would name her son after Troy Aikman.

God, no.

The little fellow continued to scream, his face an alarmingly dark shade of pink. Obviously he was hungry or had a dirty diaper or one of those things that made babies cry. Reed rocked the little seat, but baby Troy kept right on wailing. He dipped a hand between baby and seat, trying to brace himself if he should touch anything wet and warm. What he was going to do with the kid once he picked him up, he hadn't a clue. Feed him, he supposed. But what? He didn't exactly serve milk to the tourists on his cruises, and a baby couldn't drink wine.

An edge of paper hit his fingertip. Leaving the baby in place, he pulled out the paper. A note.

Please hide and protect my baby.

The note was short and sweet. The words disturbing. But even more disturbing was the familiar round and loopy curves of the script.

It was Honey's writing, all right.

A stabbing headache lodged at the back of his skull. His nausea grew until he thought he might have to race up the steps and puke over the boat's rail.

He was no judge of a baby's age, but this one couldn't be all that old. Maybe a month? No, more like two or three. And if he added either number to nine, the total came awfully close to the amount of time that had passed since he'd left Dallas…the last night he'd been with Honey.

He closed his eyes. The baby kept wailing, the sound wrapping around his throat, tightening, choking. He wasn't ready for a child. Of that he was sure. It had been only a little over a year since his mother's death. A year since he'd finally left Honey. He had just started to live his own life. He couldn't get dragged under by that kind of stifling responsibility again.

He scooped in breath after breath. He had to chill out. He had to think.

He couldn't assume this baby was his, not without knowing more. He needed some facts before he could figure out what to do next.

He looked at the note again. Protect and hide. Protect and hide. What did Honey want him to protect and hide the baby *from?* Why had she left the baby in his boat?

He eyed the baby blanket. The loopy endearment. The embroidered, personalized "Troy." Honey had carefully chosen her son's name. He had to assume she'd just as carefully chosen to leave her baby with him. And that she had to be pretty desperate to do so.

A clatter rose from above deck.

He spun around, searching the doorway, the steps leading into the cabin. Could someone be up there right now? Looking for Honey or the baby? Wanting to hurt the little guy for some unfathomable reason?

He grabbed an empty wine bottle from last night's trash. His heart knocked against his rib cage as if desperate to break through. His legs and arms jittered with adrenaline. The bottle's glass neck felt slick in his palm.

He'd been in one bar fight in his life, back in a rowdy Texas roadhouse in Springton, not far from the ranch where he'd grown up. The black eye, split lip and monster headache he'd been left with was enough to teach him to hold his temper. Maybe this time he didn't have to fight through the booze haze, but he had no idea whom he was about to face. Or why. Or how'd he got into this mess in the first place.

He slipped out of the kitchenette and approached the stairs. He breathed shallowly, quietly, trying to hear over the thunk of his heart and the baby's persistent crying. Gulls shrieked. Water lapped at the dock's pilings.

A footfall sounded on the boat's deck above. A shadow fell across the steps.

Reed raised the bottle.

Chapter Two

"Reed, honey? What in the—" Missy Donderfeldt's ample frame filled the doorway and blocked the morning sun. Dressed in her usual pink tracksuit, she plopped hands on hips and glowered at him through rimless glasses. "What on earth are you doing?"

Reed lowered his makeshift weapon. Embarrassment heated all the way to his hairline. The mysterious appearance of a baby and one little note warning to hide and protect, and Reed had almost assaulted one of the kindest and most generous people he'd ever known. "Sorry about that, Missy. I guess I'm a bit jumpy this morning."

"I can hear why. You have a baby in there?" She pushed past him and descended into the cabin. "Poor little soul sounds like he's starving to death."

Reed almost groaned. He loved Missy, but the last thing he wanted to do was explain why a baby was left in the cabin of his boat. Especially since he didn't *really* know the answer himself. Or maybe he just didn't want to face it. "I'm fine, Missy. Really, you don't need to—"

"Fine? You might be fine, but this little one sure isn't." She bustled into the kitchen area, nearly filling the cramped space. She shook her head, her graying bob swinging against her cheeks. "This child is hungry."

Reed followed her. "I don't know…"

She picked up a baby bag sitting on the floor that Reed hadn't even noticed. "Is there a bottle in here?"

"I…I don't know."

She gave him a disapproving press of the lips. "Men. You don't know much, do you?"

He knew better than to answer that.

"You go ahead and do whatever it is you were doing. I'll have this little one taken care of in a sec." She rummaged in the bag, pulled out a bottle and popped it into the microwave. When the chime rang, she pulled it out, shook it and squeezed out a drop on the inside of her wrist. "Perfect." She handed the bottle to Reed.

He looked at the strangely squared-off nipple and then at the kid.

"You want me to feed the poor little darling, too?"

Reed felt a little guilty for pawning the whole baby thing off on Missy, but that didn't keep him from nodding. She had raised four children, after all. God knew he'd heard stories about them every day. "Would you?"

"I thought you'd never ask." She expertly picked the baby out of the bucket seat, plopped herself down on one of the benches along the wall and stuck the nipple into the open little mouth.

The crying stopped. Missy smiled down at the baby as if the little guy was one of her own grandchildren. "So why do you have a baby on your boat?"

Just like that, the tightness came back, gripping his throat. "I'm still trying to figure that out."

Her normally friendly eyes narrowed. "Are you saying you just found him here?"

"Yes."

"With no idea where he came from?"

"Well…"

"Is he yours?"

"I…I don't know."

"But you think he is, don't you? I can see the fear in your eyes."

Is that what he felt at the prospect of this being his child? Fear? Maybe. But he'd describe it more as the feeling of being sucked back into living someone else's life instead of his own. "He might be mine. I don't really know."

"Who is she? The mother, I mean." She hitched her head back and studied him, glasses low on her nose. "And don't go saying you don't know. If you think this child might be yours, you must have an idea who his mother is."

He let out a breath. He might as well not even try to keep secrets from Missy. She was nothing if not perceptive, even if she was a little overbearing. "I think it might be a woman I dated before I came out here."

"Name?"

"Honey Dawson."

She looked down at the baby and smoothed her hand over the blue blanket. Her fingertips lingered on the cootchie-cootchie embroidery. "I take it his name is Troy."

He shrugged, although Missy wasn't looking at him to notice. "I need to try to reach Honey, find out what's going on."

"And you want me to take care of the child while you make the call?"

Again he felt guilty for asking, but he didn't withdraw his unspoken request. "It will just take a few minutes."

She waved him away with the back of her hand. "Go ahead. He'll be just fine here with me."

He eyed the little guy's contented sucking and the gentle way Missy cradled him. Troy would be fine, all right. Reed just wasn't sure about himself. Or about Honey. She never would have abandoned her child. Not after the way she was deserted by her own mother, without a name, without any idea of where she'd come from. No, something had happened. Something that had made her desperate enough to travel all the way to California and leave her baby with him. And the more he thought about what it could be, the more worried he became.

BOBBY WRAPPED HIS FINGERS around the hot foam cup and pretended to watch the sea lions along with the rest of the tourists. From his new vantage point, he'd seen an older woman disappear into Tanner's sailboat. And from the corner of his eye he now watched Tanner himself emerge.

The guy must have taken a very short boat trip, and Bobby wanted to know why. If only he could just walk up to Tanner and ask.

In the past hour he'd traded his rifle for a more concealable 9mm, had a nice chat with the maid who'd lied through her teeth about when Honey had left for the pier this morning and picked up the caffeine he craved. What he hadn't been able to get was satisfaction.

If Honey had already come and gone, before Reed Tanner had reached the pier this morning, he wanted to know why. It sure wasn't with the purpose of talking to her ex. She must have left something for him.

Bobby needed to find out what.

Tanner paced across the deck, a cell phone clapped tight to his ear. Calling someone. Honey? The police? Child services? Bobby couldn't answer. But he had all morning to wait and watch. And as soon as he got the chance, he would take a look inside that boat.

REED PUNCHED THE CELL phone's Off button and restrained himself from throwing the thing over the boat's rail. He'd tried every number he had for Honey. Her cell. The landline she'd apparently disconnected. The restaurant where he'd learned she no longer worked. It was as if she'd fallen off the face of the earth.

He had only one number left to try.

The phone on the other end picked up on the third ring. "Yeah. What do you want?"

From the hostile tone of Jimmy Bartow's voice, Reed figured he must have caller ID. "I'm looking for Honey."

"You should know where she is better than I do."

"Why is that?"

A heavy pause stretched over the line. "Didn't she come to see you?"

Suddenly the air felt thin, as if he could gasp and gasp and never get enough oxygen. Reed had figured only Honey would embroider a blanket with cootchie-cootchie-coo. He'd recognized her handwriting on the note. He'd thought he'd accepted the prospect that since Honey had left the baby, that meant the baby might be his. But somehow hearing all those things confirmed hit him like a boot upside the head.

"Tanner? Where's Honey?"

"She was here."

"Was? What did you do?"

The accusing tone of Bartow's voice didn't surprise him. He had no idea what Honey had told her buddy Jimmy about their breakup, but it couldn't have cast Reed in a good light. Not that Jimmy had ever liked him. Jealousy will do that to a man. "She came to the pier, but she left before I arrived. I didn't get to talk to her."

"Is she on her way back to Dallas?"

"I don't know."

"If you have a decent bone in your body, you'll stay away from her."

"I need to talk to her, Jimmy. That's all. I don't want some kind of reunion."

"You don't deserve her. You never deserved her."

What was he supposed to say to that? Reed hesitated. Should he mention the baby to Jimmy? An uneasy feeling shifted deep in his gut. No. If this child was his, it wasn't any of Jimmy's business. He needed to talk to Honey first. "If you hear from her, can you tell her to call me?"

"Go to hell, Tanner." The line went dead.

"Nice talking to you, Jimmy." Reed slapped the phone shut. Somehow he doubted Bartow would pass along the message.

"How did it go?"

Reed started at the sound of Missy's voice. For such a large woman, she was as light on her feet as a cat burglar.

She mounted the steps, the baby against her shoulder, the blue blanket pulled up around his head, shielding him from the wind. "That well?"

Reed held out a hand to help Missy onto the boat's deck. He didn't want to expose the failures of his personal life to Missy, but he supposed it was too late for that. Besides, Missy was a force of nature. He couldn't stop her prying any more than he could stop the fog rolling in over the bay. And who knew, maybe she could help. "She's not answering her cell phone. But according to a friend, she's here in San Francisco."

Holding the baby against her shoulder, Missy patted his back through the blue blanket. "I might have an idea about how to find her."

"I'm all for ideas. God knows, my brain is dry."

"First I have to know something. You still have feelings for this Honey?"

He stifled a groan. He should have known any idea Missy had would come in the form of romance counseling. She'd been trying to set him up with a niece of hers for months. So far, he'd escaped. "Listen, Missy, I know you mean well, but—"

"I don't mean anything. I just asked a question. If you don't have feelings for her, it should be pretty easy to answer."

"I don't have feelings for anyone except you, Missy. You know that." He threw in a teasing wink for good measure.

She shot him a skeptical frown. "That's only because you need me to take care of your baby."

He opened his mouth to protest that it wasn't his baby, then shut it without uttering a word. He had to straighten this out. He had to find Honey. Now. "I thought you said you had an idea."

Missy shifted the baby into one arm and dipped a hand into the giant purse she always had slung over one shoulder. "Not just an idea." She pulled out a plain-looking business card and offered it to Reed.

He peered down at the name. "J. R. Dionne?"

"A private investigator who's done work for my family in the past."

Reed looked up at Missy. He was so used to her trying to fix him up, he wasn't prepared for her to give him a tip that was not related to finding his soul mate and settling down. A tip that was actually helpful. "Thanks."

Missy nodded and looked down at the baby. "And if you hire J. R. Dionne, I'll take care of this little guy as part of the bargain. You don't mind, do you?"

"Mind? You're kidding, right? You'd be saving my life."

She held a finger in the air. "You hire J. R. Dionne, and I'm at your disposal."

Reed nodded. He didn't have a clue what stake Missy had in this private investigator, but he hoped the guy would work out. Reed might know nothing about babies, but he knew enough not to turn down free babysitting.

Chapter Three

Josie Renata Dionne had been sitting in her one-room office for less than half an hour when the best-looking man she'd seen this month pulled open the frosted glass door and peeked inside. "Excuse me, is this the private investigator's office?"

"Yes, it is."

He glanced at the wall to one side, then the other, as if looking for some kind of inner office door. Finding none, he turned his focus back to her and the nameplate on her desk.

Even though she'd been in business only a few months, one look at the guy's face, and Josie could tell he'd expected J. R. Dionne to be a man. They always did. It often gave her a chuckle to see their thinly disguised shock morph into doubt. Half the time she expected such would-be clients to spin on their heels and march right back out of her office. Half the time, they did, despite her low rates and years as a police officer.

But this one was different.

The shock was there. The arch to the strong brows. The widening of the hazel eyes, eyes she suspected would change color depending on his mood. But instead of doubt following the surprise, he smiled.

What a smile.

Her heart gave a little stutter. She didn't have a clue what to say.

"You're J. R. Dionne?"

"Um, yes."

"I should have known." He pushed the door wide and stepped inside.

Dressed in jeans and a sporty jacket, he moved with a casual ease she couldn't quite place. But wherever he'd picked it up, it was sexy as hell. She glanced at his hand. No ring. She pulled her gaze immediately back to his face. "Should have known what?"

"Nothing." He met her gaze directly. Another thing that set him apart. Most men couldn't get their eyes to focus on anything above her frustratingly ample chest. Back in her years as a cop, even the badge hadn't distracted them.

He must be gay. "What can I help you with?"

"I need to find someone."

"Who?"

"An old girlfriend."

Okay, so maybe not gay. Just not available. She knew something was wrong with him. Something had to be. "When did you see her last?"

"Almost a year ago. I haven't talked to her. I just learned she was coming to San Francisco to see me, but she never showed."

Almost a year? Haven't talked to her? That didn't sound very taken. Maybe she hadn't imagined the way he looked at her, the shimmer that had shot up her spine when he gave her that megawatt grin. "So you want me to find her?"

"Yes."

"What's her name?"

"Before we start, can I ask what your rates are?"

She pushed a rate sheet across her desk. So he wasn't so wealthy that price wasn't a problem. She could deal with that small flaw. She was starting to get greedy, anyway.

He picked up the paper and stared at it for an uncomfortably long time.

"Do you have any questions?" she prompted.

He looked up from the paper and focused on her with an intensity that made her nerves dance. "Can you start right away?"

"I just finished a big insurance case, so my calendar is relatively clear." Who was she kidding? Her calendar was uncomfortably empty and so was her pocketbook. But somehow, money wasn't the most attractive part of this case.

She bit her lip. She had to keep herself in check. As nice as her imaginings were, romantic relationships didn't work out for her. Never had. Either the guy disappointed her or he got cold feet when it came to commitment, but it was always something. Before Mr. Gorgeous had walked in the door, she'd given up all hope of romance, and a hot smile wasn't enough reason to reconsider.

But man, she was having fun with the fantasy, and she couldn't quite shake the hope that it might become more.

"I'd like to hire you, then."

"Okay. Why don't you tell me a little bit about your situation?"

"Like what? Oh, yeah, her name. Honey. Honey Dawson."

"Honey? You're kidding, right?"

He smiled and gave a little shrug.

"Her parents must have had some kind of taste."

"No parents. She was found in Dawson County, Georgia. The social workers named her Honey for the color of her hair."

She groaned inside. Talk about inserting foot in mouth. Being around good-looking men was dangerous, and this one was worse than most. He made her blood feel a little too bubbly, her tongue too loose. "I'm sorry for being flip."

"Don't worry about it."

Again with that smile. She felt tingly, maybe a little drunk. The last time she'd felt this off-center around a man was…never.

There had to be something not perfect about this guy, something she was missing. There always was. "Maybe you should tell me why you're interested in finding Honey Dawson before this goes any further." Had she just said that? Heat centered in her cheeks. Man, she was slick, wasn't she? "I just don't want to waste our time…or your money…if I can help it."

He nodded. "I'm worried she's in trouble."

"Trouble? What makes you think she's in trouble?"

He glanced at his watch, a sturdy number, more practical than flashy. "I think it would be easier to show you than explain. My boat is down at the wharf."

"Your boat?"

"A catamaran. I provide cruises on the bay."

This was looking up all the time. Since she still didn't

know his name, maybe she should call him Captain Gorgeous. She laughed to herself.

He frowned. "Is that funny?"

"No. No. I was just thinking earlier how much fun it would be to take a cruise. I've never done that."

"If you'll come with me, I can take you out after I show you what she left on my boat."

Take her out. She liked where this was going. Still, there had to be something wrong. There always was. "What did she leave on your boat?"

"A baby."

A shock traveled from Josie's ears to her toes. "Excuse me? Did you say a baby?"

"Yup. A baby."

A baby. Just the word started up that empty throb in her chest. "*Your* baby?"

"I...I don't know. All I know is that Honey left him with me."

Josie let her eyes wander over that dark, wavy hair one more time. She took in the bright hazel of his eyes, more on the green side now. She imagined touching the stubble on his jaw, tasting the warmth of his lips, falling asleep to the music of his voice and waking up to that smile.

Or waking up to the cry of a baby. A cry just for her.

She shook her head, jolting herself out of the fantasy. She needed to step back, not let her imagination go overboard. This couldn't actually be happening. There had to be something wrong with this guy. "Could I ask you where you got my name?"

"A friend referred you. She said you've done work for her family."

A bad feeling clamped down on the back of Josie's neck. "Would her name happen to be Missy Donderfeldt?"

"Well, yes."

She should have known. He had just the look she liked. Just the right build. And the baby… For a woman who'd been waiting to adopt as long as she had, the baby put him way over the top. This was matchmaking if she'd ever experienced it, and with Missy for an aunt, she'd experienced it a lot. "Tanner. You're Reed Tanner. The one who has coffee with her every morning before she opens the shop."

The pieces seemed to be falling into place in his mind, too. She could recognize it in the sardonic smile playing at one corner of his lips. "And I'll bet the *J* stands for Josie. You're Missy's niece."

"She's told you about me before?"

He nodded.

Of course she had. And she'd told Josie about him, too. She'd told her far too much.

What had her aunt been thinking? She knew what kind of a man Reed Tanner was. She'd told Josie the stories of how he'd moved to the bay area to run away from responsibility. To avoid settling down. And now Missy had gotten it into her head that she should set him up with Josie? Just when Josie was getting her life together? Just when she was inching closer to getting everything she wanted? "I'm sorry, Mr. Tanner. My aunt never should have referred you to me. I can't take your case."

He gave his head a little shake, as if convinced his ears weren't working quite right. "You have to take the case."

"I can give you another name. Someone reputable."

"Is it the baby?"

The baby? Of course it was the baby. And her hormones and the fact that just being around him made her feel drunk. "It has nothing to do with the baby."

"Your aunt has promised to take care of him. At least, she has as long as I hire you."

Josie fought the urge to groan. So that was why he was so eager. Wait until she gave Missy a chunk of her mind. "The baby is fine. It's not that."

"Then what's the problem?"

It's being around you. She glanced down at her appointment book. "I just…don't have time. I'm overbooked."

"You didn't think that was a problem when I came in."

"I didn't think your case would be so…involved then."

"And you think it's involved now? We haven't even talked about it."

"Abandoned children always make things more involved."

He held up a hand. "Listen, Honey has her problems, but she never would have abandoned her baby."

Oh, that made her feel so much better. Not. She massaged the back of her neck. She was coming down with a monster headache.

"I'm worried about her. I think she might be in some kind of trouble. I need your help."

"That's what the police are for. If you really feel she's in trouble, you should call them."

"And tell them what? You know they can't do anything unless she's been missing for a while. I doubt they have the manpower to do much then. I don't even know when she arrived in San Francisco or if she's still here now."

"So you don't know if she's really missing. Maybe she'll turn up. Maybe everything will be fine."

"Or maybe it won't." His eyes grew darker, all pupil with a vivid green rim.

She shifted in her seat. She hated to turn away someone in need, but she just couldn't be around this guy. She was too attracted to him. Too tempted. She didn't need to set herself up for a broken heart.

She opened her card file and shuffled through until she found what she was looking for. "Call this office and ask for Brian Wilmer. He'll do a great job for you, and his rates are better than mine."

He took the card but didn't spare it a glance. "Listen, if you don't want to take my case, that's fine. But like I said, Missy offered to babysit as long as I hired you to look for Honey, and…"

It was a guess, but she thought she knew where he was headed. "And you'd like me to tell her I was the one who turned you down?"

"Would you mind? I'll throw in a free cruise on the bay." He glanced at his watch once more. "I have one scheduled in less than an hour."

"You want me to go with you right now?"

"I'm a little desperate here."

A desperate and good-looking bachelor who refused to settle down. With a baby, for crying out loud. God help her. When she caught up with Missy, she was going to wring her aunt's neck.

REED UNLOCKED THE GATE leading to Dock J and ushered Josie Dionne through. He'd made an afternoon appointment with the investigator she'd referred, and for the rest of the awkward cab ride down the city's hills and one-way streets, he'd been at a loss for things to say. Now he felt like a clueless teenage boy trying to impress her with his chivalry.

What had gotten into him?

Normally he was good at small talk. It was part of his cruise business's success. But with all that had gone down this morning, his usual fodder of restaurants and weather seemed trite. And since she'd refused his case, he'd prefer to avoid chatting about the concerns that were really on his mind.

Too bad.

If he had known *this* was the woman that Missy wanted to set him up with, he would have taken her up on her offer a long time ago. Josie's short, swingy blond hair, high cheekbones and twinkling blue eyes were a pleasure to look at. Not to mention that body. Slender, fit and a chest straight out of a man's dreams. But even more striking than the way she looked was the way she seemed so…in control. At ease with herself. Focused. A woman who wouldn't be needy or clingy. The requirement at the top of his list.

"So which one is it?" Josie motioned to the handful of boats moored in their slips along the dock.

He snapped his thoughts back to reality. His most important concern now was to retain Missy as a babysitter, not catalog Josie's attributes. Attributes he wouldn't have a chance to enjoy anyway. "The catamaran on the end."

"The big one?"

Pride wriggled deep in his chest. "That's her."

"She's beautiful."

"Thanks." His boat wasn't actually all that big, but

it was a beauty. And she'd cost a pretty penny. "I can take up to about twenty passengers."

"Always wanted to sail?"

"Yes, ma'am. Just me and the water and the wind."

She gave him a dry look he wasn't sure how to read and waited for him to unlock the second gate.

He waved her through to the steps rising to the sailboat's deck. "Missy is in the cabin with the baby."

She climbed the steps to the sailboat's deck, Reed following. For a second he allowed himself to watch her hips sway in front of him. What the hell? Might as well enjoy himself while he could.

At the top of the stairs he offered his hand, helping her keep her balance as she stepped onto the boat. He pointed to the door leading down into the cabin. "Hey, Missy. I brought someone here to say hi."

He could see a dark shape stir through the open door, but no answer came from his impromptu babysitter. "Missy?" He narrowed his eyes, willing them to adjust after the glare of the sun outside.

The dark shape rushed at him. Before he could think, before he could react, it plowed into him.

He fell backward. Reaching out, he gripped a jean-clad leg and held on.

A blow landed against the side of his head. Pain rattled through his skull and ricocheted down his spine. He tightened his grip on the intruder's leg. The man hulked above him. Long, dark gray coat. Blond hair. And in his arms he held something wrapped in a baby-blue blanket.

Chapter Four

Josie didn't think, she just lunged. Her fingers closed around the man's biceps. He yanked his arm back, throwing her off balance. His coat sleeve slipped against the hard muscle of his arm.

The baby's frightened shriek filled her ears.

She dug in her fingernails and struggled to hold on. She couldn't let him get away. She brought up her other hand, raking her fingers, trying to reach his face, his eyes.

He dodged her flailing hand. He yanked his arm. The sleeve slipped from her grasp. He brought his fist crashing down on her shoulder. Her legs crumpled beneath her and she hit the boat's deck.

Moving to run, the man stumbled.

"Grab the baby," Reed yelled. He lay on the deck, his arms wrapped around the man's legs.

The man thrashed against his hold. He pulled back a leg and thunked the hard toe of a cowboy boot into Reed's chest.

Scrambling to her feet, Josie focused on the man's face. Blond hair. Ruddy skin. Piggish eyes. She went straight for his eyes. Her fingers hit flesh, jabbing into soft tissue.

A bellow came from the man. His hands flew to his face.

The baby.

Josie jumped forward, arms outstretched. Her hands closed around the little body just as both of them hit the hard fiberglass of the deck.

Air whooshed from her lungs. The fall reverberated through her bones. She struggled to breathe, but could manage nothing more than empty gasps.

She felt his hands on her body. Grabbing her. Shoving her. He drew back a boot, preparing to kick.

Reed came up swinging. The guy stumbled back. Reed went after him, thrusting himself between the man and Josie.

A splitting ache pounded through her skull. She didn't know how much time passed. Two seconds. Two minutes. It didn't matter. All that mattered was protecting the baby in her arms. All that mattered was making him safe. She ran her hands over the little guy. He was still screaming, but he didn't seem hurt, not that she could tell.

Heavy footfalls vibrated down the boat's steps and thundered on the wooden planks of the pier below.

Suddenly Reed was bending over her. "Josie, are you—"

"I'm fine. Stop him. Go."

His hands moved over the crying baby, then touched Josie's cheek. "Are you sure?"

"Go." Josie struggled to a sitting position. Unwrapping the little face, she checked the baby further. He seemed okay. Miraculously fine.

She twisted toward the pier. The man had vaulted the

first gate and had already reached the second. Reed thundered down the pier toward him, but checking her had taken time. Too much time. In seconds the man would blend into the crowd milling around shops and restaurants. Finding him would be like isolating a shard of glass in a beach of white sand.

A couple strolled along the pier. They drew even with the gate.

"Stop that man," Reed yelled. "Stop him."

The couple looked past the man and stared at Reed. The man circled his arm around the woman's shoulders and hurried her away. The man who had attacked her disappeared into the crowd of bodies. Reed plunged after him, but Josie knew he'd never catch up. Whoever the guy was, whatever reason he had for kidnapping a baby, the man was gone.

Josie's head whirled. Stroking the baby's fuzz of hair, she quieted him and tried to think. The man had seemed to come from nowhere. How had she not seen him before he'd attacked?

She'd been distracted, that's how. Not paying atten-tion. She'd been focused on Reed and that damn fizz of attraction in her bloodstream. She'd been caught up in her anger with Missy for setting her up with the most inappropriate man in the…

Where was Missy?

Josie's heart stuttered. Holding the baby tight to her shoulder, she thrust herself up to her knees, to her feet. She half stumbled down the steps and into the relative dimness of the cabin. Her aunt had to be here. She had to be okay. "Missy?"

A small sound, like a light sniffing, came from the

galley-style kitchenette. Josie hurried toward the sound. She rounded the countertop.

Missy lay on her side on the vinyl floor. Blood matted her hair and ran down the side of her face.

Josie stifled a gasp. Holding the baby with one hand, she knelt and touched her aunt's cheek. "Missy?"

She didn't move.

Josie moved shaking fingers over her jaw and to the soft tissue of her throat. Her skin was warm. The tick of a pulse tapped Josie's fingertips.

She fumbled in her bag for her cell phone. Hand shaking, she flipped the phone open with one hand, punched in 911 and prayed.

THE HOSPITAL SMELLS and sounds beat at him like an ambulance's pulsing siren. If he let them, they would take him back to the dark days and weeks he'd spent in Dallas hospitals, days when he felt like he was drowning in guilt and worry, the days before his mother's death. But even though he refused to go there, he couldn't keep those same feelings from lapping at the back of his mind. Missy Donderfeldt, one of the sweetest people he'd ever known, was in serious condition. And he had to wonder if he was partly to blame.

"Reed." A strong feminine voice sounded from behind him.

He turned to face Josie Dionne. Eyes red and makeup long since cried off, she cradled Troy against her chest, the baby fast asleep. He hadn't seen her since she'd accompanied Missy while he'd stayed at the boat to talk to police. She'd insisted on taking the baby with her, clutching him as if she'd needed to hold something while the paramedics worked on her aunt. Now she stood ramrod straight, a determined press to her jaw.

"How's Missy doing?" he asked.

"They say she's stable. But she hasn't regained consciousness. My mom is with her now."

Was that where the determination came from? Holding it together for her family? A woman set on handling whatever came at her and taking care of others to boot. She struck him as that type. Not that he'd known many.

"Did you just get here?"

He nodded. "It took a while."

"Did the police find anything?"

Good question. He'd been with them for hours, and he still couldn't answer. "If they did, they didn't share it with me." He wished Josie could have stayed at the boat. Missy had told him she used to be a cop. They might have been more open with her, told her something. Not that he would have traded places with her at the hospital. Not for damn sure.

"They told you nothing?"

"All they would give me is some line about a burglar in the area."

Her eyebrows arched upward. "A burglar who steals babies?"

"Maybe you can talk to them."

"I did."

"They didn't tell you anything? Missy said you were once a police officer."

"I was, but no. I don't think they have much to tell. And I didn't help. A weak description. That's about all I could give them."

He knew the feeling. Everything had happened so

fast, he was still trying to sort it out in his mind. But he had a few ideas. "So they sent someone to talk to you already?"

An orderly wheeled a patient past them. A nurse scurried down the hall in the opposite direction, the rubber soles of her shoes squeaking lightly on the waxed floor.

Reed waited until the nurse passed. He wasn't one given to paranoia, but he didn't want anyone overhearing their business. After the attack, he felt more vulnerable than he had since he was a kid. But this was different. Worse in a way, because he not only needed to protect himself, but Troy and Josie and Missy, as well. Scratch that. He'd already failed Missy. "Is there a waiting room or somewhere we can go and talk about this?"

"Sure, but the waiting room is pretty full."

"Somewhere else?"

She motioned for him to follow. Reaching an exit sign, she pushed open the door beneath and led him into the stairwell. The door thunked closed behind them. "You know something, don't you? Who was that man? What did he want?" She stared at him as if waiting for him to explain everything.

He blew out a heavy breath. "I don't know."

"Why would he want a baby?"

"Maybe he doesn't. Maybe he wants Honey, and the baby is just a way to get to her."

"You told the police that?"

"Yes. Although I don't think I did a good job of convincing them. They didn't even seem to take the note all that seriously."

"The note?"

He'd forgotten. He'd never told Josie about the note.

After she'd turned down the case, he'd no longer had a reason. "Honey left a note tucked in the baby's seat."

She stepped toward him and stuck out her free hand. "Can I see it?"

"I gave it to the police."

"What did it say?"

"'Please hide and protect my baby.'"

She gave a sullen nod, as if absorbing the words. "That's all?"

"Yes. She didn't even sign it, although I know her writing."

"What did Brian think?"

"Brian?"

"The P.I. I referred you to."

"Damn." He glanced at his watch. "I should have met with him an hour ago."

"So you haven't hired him?"

"No."

"Good. I want to take the case. That is, if you still want me. I'll even throw in babysitting."

Her turnaround didn't really surprise him. Apparently there was more to that determined set to her jaw than being strong for the family. Josie was ready for a fight. "You've got a deal."

"You're not going to ask why I changed my mind?"

The answer seemed more than obvious to him. "Your aunt was attacked. You want to find out who did it. If he is really after Honey, finding her means finding answers."

She nodded, although the way she averted her eyes suggested there might be more she wasn't saying. "And you're okay with that?"

"Why wouldn't I be? I want to find out who hurt

Missy, too. If it wasn't for me, she never would have been in my boat with the baby. I feel responsible."

Her gaze flicked to him, then away.

That was it. That look. The way she averted her eyes. "You feel responsible, too. Why?"

She shook her head. "Not responsible. Not really. Just…guilty."

"Why would you feel guilty?"

She shook her head again. "I was angry with her. That's all. I went with you to give her a piece of my mind. And now…" She looked down at the floor and patted the baby's back, as if Troy was the one who needed comforting.

"She'll be okay. She will." Reed touched the sleeve of her jacket. A soft touch, no more than a brush of the fingertips, but he meant it with every cell in his body.

Josie raised her eyes to his. "She has to be."

He couldn't agree more. He'd let too many people down in his life. He couldn't let Missy down, too. "And between the police and us, we'll find this guy. Before he hurts anyone else."

She cupped her chin toward the fat little cheek resting on her shoulder. "I sure hope so."

JOSIE DIDN'T EXPECT many favors from her little brother. She never had. But she'd expected more than this. "I just need you to tell me if—"

"You know better than to ask me questions like that." The reproach in his voice hurt more than a sharp slap.

"Normally I wouldn't. But this is urgent."

"As urgent as me keeping my job?"

Josie shifted on the edge of the bed. After all she'd

done for him. She let out a sigh. Chuckie wouldn't even have that job if not for her urging. She'd supported him and prodded him in everything he'd ever done, and this was the thanks she got. Him acting as if she were trying to screw him over. She should have known when he didn't show up for the party celebrating the opening of her own detective agency that he didn't feel obligated to return any favors she'd done him. She shook her head at her own drama. Chuckie didn't have a problem with her quitting the force or hanging out her shingle as a P.I. It was the reason she'd done it he didn't agree with.

Maybe she should have gone to see him in person. Not at the airport where he worked, but at home where his guard would be down. He certainly would have found it harder to turn her down face-to-face. "I just want to know if she flew on your airline. And when she arrived from Dallas. She's the mother of a baby. She's missing."

"If she's missing, call the police."

"I've already talked to the police. You know they don't have the manpower to track down a woman who has only been gone a few hours." According to Reed, it was questionable whether they even saw a connection to the man who'd hurt Missy. "She's in trouble."

"Better than me being in trouble."

"There's more."

"I'm hanging up now."

"I think this is connected with the attack on Missy."

"What?"

"The guy who hurt her. He was after Honey Dawson's baby. Or maybe Honey Dawson herself."

"Call the police, Josie. If they get a warrant for the information, then I can give it to them."

"They don't—"

"Them. Not you. If you wanted that power, you should have stayed a cop. I have to go." The line went dead.

Josie stabbed the Off button on the cordless phone. So much for connections and shortcuts. Her brother hadn't forgiven her for quitting the force. He didn't understand that she wanted to be in control of her own life. And he didn't approve of her reason. Or at least, he thought she was getting the natural order of things mixed up. He thought she should be married before she became a mother.

Whatever. She wouldn't disagree with him…if this were a perfect world. But it wasn't. And she'd had it with banking her future on men who couldn't commit or love she couldn't trust. She wanted to control her own life.

Unfortunately her brother's refusal to help left her relying on good old-fashioned legwork to find Honey. And there were a sea of hotels in San Francisco that she needed to cover. She lowered herself to the corner of the queen-size mattress on a plain frame. The room looked like it belonged to a bachelor, all right. Rumpled sheets and tangled blankets. Bare walls. No furniture but the bed and a chest of drawers that had seen many coats of now-chipping paint. Not her idea of an adult's bedroom. Not her idea of a functional office in which to work, either, but less distracting than sitting out in the living room with the baby and the television…and Reed.

He'd nearly begged her to come back to his apartment, to stay the night. Some sex-starved, hormone-driven part of her wanted to think he'd extended the invitation with hopes of passion igniting between them, but she knew the truth. He was afraid of being alone with the baby.

She supposed she had to give him credit for convincing the police that Honey had left the baby in his care and there was no need for child protective services to take over. He had even arranged for a medical exam while they were at the hospital, to make sure the baby was okay. But when it came to actually caring for little Troy, he seemed scared to death. Or maybe that part just took too much commitment and responsibility for him to handle. When she'd left to make the call to her brother, he'd been across the room from where she'd put the baby on a blanket on the floor, as if wary about getting too close. When she returned, he was in the same spot. "I need your help."

"Sure."

Troy lifted his head from the blanket and gave her a gassy little smile.

She knelt down and kissed his head, pulling the scent of baby shampoo deep. He sure seemed well cared for. From his personalized blanket to his freshly washed hair, Troy seemed to have a mommy who loved him. A mommy it was up to her to find. "I need to know more about Honey."

"What about her?"

"First, do you have a picture of her?"

"Just a second." He walked past her and disappeared into the bedroom. A few moments later he returned with a photo album. He flipped open the cover and handed the binder to her.

The first page featured snapshots of a gorgeous

honey blonde. Tiny shorts hugged trim hips. Her belly stretched bare and washboard flat. The cropped skin-tight top showed off the perfect amount of cleavage. A combination of athletic, sexy and glamorous with just the smallest touch of girl next door.

It was depressing.

"There are more in there. Ones where she's wearing normal clothes. If you want to take one, go ahead."

Josie flipped the page. More photos of the stunning blonde stared back at her. Honey laughing. Honey sitting on a fence. Honey looking every bit as sexy in jeans and a T-shirt as she had in the skimpy outfit. "You have a whole scrapbook of her?"

"She made it for me when I moved. She said she didn't want me to forget her."

Josie almost guffawed out loud. As if that were likely. Josie couldn't imagine any man forgetting *that*.

She slipped a snapshot free. She needed to get a grip. Focus on why she was here. She should find Honey's looks encouraging. It would be mighty hard for anyone who'd merely passed her on the street not to notice. Her looks would make Josie's job of finding her that much easier. But somehow handing the album back to Reed just made her want to fold her arms across her oversized chest and flabby middle and hide.

"Anything else?"

Josie took a deep breath and pushed her insecurities back from where they'd crawled. "Has she ever been to San Francisco before?"

"She was here with me before I moved. When I bought the boat."

Great. Now if Josie wanted to be really pitiful, she

could dwell on all the happy memories of Captain Gorgeous and the perfect woman right here in her hometown. "Where did you stay?"

"A friend's apartment."

"Where exactly?"

"Actually, this is the place. He moved, and I took over his lease."

So much for the possibility that Honey had holed up somewhere she'd stayed before. "What areas of the city did the two of you visit?"

"I don't know. We did the usual tourist things. We were only here a few days."

"What things specifically?"

"The wharf, of course, and Alcatraz. Golden Gate Park. We ate at Cliff House. That's about it, I guess."

"What was her favorite?"

"That's easy. Shopping."

"Shopping? Where?" There were a myriad of places to shop in San Francisco. The where of it all depended on what one wanted to buy.

"She did a lot of window shopping in the Union Square area. But her budget was more Chinatown."

"Okay, that's in one area of the city. Now we're getting somewhere."

"You think she's staying near Union Square and Chinatown?"

"It's likely. People usually stay in the places they're familiar with. Especially a woman traveling alone with a baby." Josie tried to think of the hotels in the areas Reed mentioned. All the ones that came to mind were pretty pricey. "You mentioned her budget. How much money might she have to spend on a hotel room?"

"I don't know. Back when we were together, she was barely making ends meet. But right before I left, she seemed to have found a source of money."

She couldn't help but notice the way his voice dipped, as if he was embarrassed to acknowledge what that source might be. But she could guess. "You mean a sugar daddy?"

He gave a shrug that seemed a bit abrupt. "After I told her I was moving, she started seeing other guys."

"She told you this?" If he had names, maybe they could figure out who had reason to come after Honey, or to come after the baby and, by default, Missy. "Do you know who?"

"No. Nothing like that. She didn't say a word to me. Kind of did it behind my back. Truth was, we both knew it was over."

"So how do you know there were others?"

"She suddenly had things. Jewelry. Clothes. Things she couldn't afford on the amount of money she was making." Another shrug, too stiff to be believable. "Even though Honey didn't make the final cut and get on the cheerleading squad, she was still one of the finalists. Having a cheerleader on your arm in Dallas is a big deal. Cheerleaders attract a lot of guys."

She'd bet Honey attracted a lot of guys whether she was a cheerleader or not. "Attractive women also attract enemies."

Reed looked at her as if he'd never considered that before. "Enemies?"

"Did Honey have any rivals?"

"Tiffany Maylor. She was a cheerleader. Rich family. She said things that really upset Honey."

"Like what?"

"I don't remember. Mean things. Trying to humiliate Honey. Intimidate her. It just about killed Honey when Tiffany made the final cut and she didn't."

"Okay, Tiffany. Who else?"

He rubbed a hand over his face. "Man, I don't have a clue."

"She didn't talk about anyone else?"

"No. She didn't have a lot of friends who were women, but she didn't have a lot of enemies, either. I suppose if her sugar daddy had a girlfriend or was married, there might be a problem there. But I can't help with that. I have no idea who was giving her those gifts."

"Is there anyone else who would want to hurt her? People who had bothered her in the past?"

"Damn."

"What?"

"I don't know why I didn't think of him. Honey had herself a stalker."

Now they were getting somewhere. "Tell me about him."

"He was a damn Peeping Tom, always looking in her windows, following her. He was annoying, but he really didn't seem dangerous until he broke into her apartment."

"He broke in? Did he try to hurt her?"

Reed shook his head. "He broke in when she wasn't there. Stole some of her underwear."

A shiver skittered up Josie's spine.

"Sick, eh?"

"What happened?"

"The police caught him. Charged him with burglary. He made a deal with the prosecutor, but Honey had to go to a bunch of hearings to testify he was the same guy who was following her. I think he prolonged it so he could see her."

"So he's still serving time?"

"I don't know."

That would be easy enough to check. "Do you have a name?"

"I want to say Kinney. Neil Kinney. To check up on Tiffany Maylor and Neil Kinney, do you have to go to Dallas?"

"Maybe. Maybe not. I'm not licensed in Texas, so if I go it would have to be as a private citizen." She held up a hand. "But we're getting a little ahead of ourselves. If we can find Honey here in San Francisco, we'll probably be able to get our answers a bit sooner."

"Well, let's hope for that. I'm all for soon." He glanced at the baby.

"You know, there are ways to find out if Troy is yours."

"You're talking about DNA?"

Obviously taking a paternity test had already occurred to him. She nodded. "I know a guy who works for a private lab that does that kind of thing. He might rush the results through as a favor."

"That would be great." His voice arched upward with hope. "If you could set that up, I'd really appreciate it."

She looked back down at Troy. The little guy's body twisted in an awkward attempt to roll over. "Funny. If someone told me Troy might be mine, I'd take it as fact and never give him back. And here you can't wait to get rid of him." She knew she shouldn't have said it, but she wasn't going to take it back. She'd do a lot for the chance to adopt a sweet baby like Troy. She had already done a lot, even though it seemed she was no closer to being a mother than she'd ever been.

"I'm…I'm not really a family guy. I'd only let him down."

Josie nodded. That was what she needed to hear. The antidote to the jealous poison that had seeped into her the moment she saw Honey's impossibly gorgeous face and figure. Reed wasn't a family guy, and was more than willing to throw away the chance to be the father of this perfect little boy. As long as she remembered that, working side by side with him to find Honey would be fine. Even sleeping in the same apartment would be a piece of cake. Because as attracted as she was to him, he could never give her what she really wanted. She'd be far better off on her own. Waiting. As long as it took.

Now if she could get through this case without telling him exactly what she thought of his attitude, that would be the true miracle.

Chapter Five

Reed cracked an eye open and growled at the morning sunlight streaming between the blind slats. He hadn't gone to sleep until the sky had already started to pink. Judging from the slant of the rays, that was hours ago.

The combination of the baby, the attack on Missy, and Josie Dionne sleeping in his bed…alone…had given him a hell of a case of insomnia. All night he'd been reliving what had happened on his boat, trying to figure out what he could have done differently. And in the end, he'd come up with nothing. But that didn't change the fact that he'd put one of the sweetest women he'd ever known in jeopardy. Because no matter what the police said about there being many explanations for the attack, he knew it was related to Honey's visit. It was all about that baby who might be his.

And then there was Josie Dionne. He could hear her moving around the kitchen now, probably heating formula for the baby. She wasn't really his type. Not tall. Not glamorous, like Honey. And most of all, independent. He'd never met a woman who was so together. She seemed as if she didn't need him at all. And that made her sexier than any cheerleader. But although he was pretty sure she was attracted to him, there was something else there, too. A disapproval he could sense. And he felt himself caring about her good opinion more than he should.

He propped himself up on his elbows to see what had made the sound. Or who. Josie stood at the stove, looking fresh and far more ready for the day than he was. So that's what had awakened him.

He forced himself to sit up on the couch. The sleeping bag he was wrapped in fell to his waist, as if he were some sort of moth shucking his cocoon. "Sleep okay?"

"Yes." She looked up at him. Her eyes widened slightly, then combed over his bare chest. "Um, you?"

"Fine," he lied. He was glad she hadn't looked at him like that last night. He wouldn't have gotten any sleep at all. Even now he was going to have to wait a few minutes for his blood to settle before he stood up. "How long have you been awake?"

"A couple of hours. My phone is dead, and I forgot my charger. I used your phone to call my mom. I hope you don't mind."

"Of course not. I did just about kidnap you to help me with the baby last night. I owe you more than your fee." He spread his arms in an all-encompassing gesture. "Whatever I have is yours."

Her gaze skimmed down his chest to the sleeping bag; then she looked away.

He hadn't meant the comment to be suggestive, not at first. But he had no problem standing by the invitation. Still, he'd better play it a little safer until he figured out where she was coming from. He needed her help, and making her feel uncomfortable was not the way to get it. "Did your mother have any news about Missy?"

Josie looked at him again. The relieved smile on her face told the whole story. "She regained consciousness late last night. She's in a room now. They think she'll probably be released tomorrow or the next day."

He was sure his grin resembled hers. "That's great."

"She's going to stay with my parents, so she won't be alone. The attack really shook her up." She let out a breath.

The attack had shaken Josie, too. And him. "Have the police told her anything?"

"No. Not that she shared with me, anyway. But she was so beside herself with worry about how she was going to pay the hospital bill and who was going to run her shop, she didn't get into much else."

"She doesn't have insurance?"

"She has it, but it doesn't cover much, as it turns out."

He hated thinking of Missy having to wrestle with finances when her focus should be on recovering from the attack. There had to be something he could do. "I just have to jump in the shower and make a few calls, and we can get out of here." He pushed the sleeping bag down his legs and stepped out. The air felt cool against his bare legs.

Josie's gaze skimmed over his boxers. Then she turned away as if fascinated with the hands on her watch. "Good. You have an appointment to get swabbed in an hour."

He grabbed his sweatpants from the chair where he'd tossed them and pulled them on before she could notice what havoc her latest glance had caused. "Swabbed?"

"It's not a big deal. They'll run a cotton swab on the

inside of your cheek and the baby's. Then they compare the DNA."

And he would know if he was a free man or his life had changed forever. "How long will the results take?"

"Hard to tell. My friend said he'd try to rush it, but it's still likely to take quite a while. Maybe weeks."

"Even a day seems too long."

The corners of Josie's mouth turned down. She tilted her chin back and peered down her nose.

He could feel the chill across the room. "So I'm not eager to be a parent yet. What's the problem?"

"No problem."

"I can feel the ice in your stare from here."

"I don't know what you're talking about."

"You were looking at me all hot, and then the kid comes up and blam. You can't stand to be in the same room as me."

"I wasn't looking at you all hot."

He shook his head. He'd said too much. Way too much. But since he'd already crossed the line, there was no reason to stop now. "You don't have to be afraid to tell me how you feel."

"How I feel?" Her tone took on a knife's edge. "Okay, I'll tell you how I feel."

He took a deep breath, already starting to regret his remark.

"I feel it's stupid for you to be so afraid of a baby. I feel Troy deserves to have a daddy, even if that daddy finds having a baby not convenient. I feel like you should grow up and show some responsibility. Be a man."

He held up his hands. He regretted it, all right. "It's not as simple as you make it seem."

"Oh? You make a baby. You do right by him. How is that not simple?"

"First off, we don't know that he's mine."

"Honey trusted you with him. He's your responsibility whether he's your son or not."

She had him there. "And I'm taking that seriously."

"By getting Missy to take care of him? And now me?"

At the mention of Missy, he felt a niggle of guilt deep in his gut. "I know when I'm in over my head. I needed help. I asked. And you and your aunt were kind enough to come to my rescue. If I'd known someone was after the baby, I'd never have left Missy alone with him."

She didn't answer, but judging from the flat line of her lips, she wasn't changing her mind about him, either.

He'd let a lot of people down in his life. He should be used to it. But Josie didn't know him. And her reaction had him baffled. She'd seemed to like him one minute and come at him like a lioness the next. He had to wonder what he'd done to cause it. "I don't know why you feel so strongly about—"

"I'd suggest you get your mind on Honey, not on how I feel. After we stop at the lab and the hospital, we'll retrace her steps. And we need a place to start." She grabbed the bottle, plunked herself on a bar stool and started feeding the baby.

Reed stared at the back of Josie's head. He knew she'd ordered his mind off her feelings. But right now that was the only place it wanted to go. He didn't know this woman. Hadn't even met her until yesterday. Yet her obviously shabby opinion of him chafed like sand against tender skin.

And he needed to figure out how to change that. "I think we've gotten off on the wrong foot here."

She didn't turn around.

"Is there something I can say to smooth things over? I'm trying."

"You're just concerned that I'm angry, that I'll leave and you won't have anyone to take care of the baby."

"Look, maybe that's part of it, but not all. I don't understand why you're so angry."

"Not angry. Sad. Disappointed. Frustrated."

He still wasn't putting it all together. "Why?"

"He might be your child. Your son. And yet you act like if you ignore him, he'll just go away."

"And he might not be mine."

"So? That's not the point."

"I guess I'm still not getting what the point is, exactly."

"If he is your son, you're missing out on something precious. Something other people would give everything for."

"Something? Okay, I'll bite. What?"

"Spending time with him. Memories. Moments together."

"We're together right now."

"No. He and I are together. You're standing on the fringes watching."

He had to admit, the way she held Troy and talked to him, the way he looked up at her with those huge eyes while sucking on his bottle, they did seem like they were together. More together than he'd been with anyone in his life. But there was one thing that Josie didn't understand. "It's not that I don't want to. I just can't."

She spun the bar stool around and looked at him as if he'd just spoken gibberish.

"For you it's easy, being with him like that. Connecting with a baby. With another person. For me…"

"How do you know if you've never tried?"

"I've tried." He'd tried with all his heart, and he'd failed. And that was not a pain he cared to relive. Or share.

"With Honey?"

"No, not with Honey." He hadn't even realized how little he'd tried with Honey. Not until Josie had asked about the details of Honey's life and he hadn't been able to give her much for answers. It wasn't that he thought more effort on his part would have changed things between him and Honey. Whatever it was that kept people together just wasn't there between them. But he regretted not being able to give her what she really needed. Love. Security. Things she hadn't enjoyed her entire life.

"So if you didn't try with Honey, then who?"

He didn't want to talk about this. Even the thought of saying the words made his stomach ache, like it had when he was a kid. "Not important. Let's just say it was long before Honey. I'm not good at connecting. That's that."

She shook her head. "Get over yourself. If this is your child, he needs you. And if he's not, he still needs you. Until we find Honey, you're all he has."

"He has you."

Her eyes narrowed. Lines dug into her forehead. Her mouth flattened to a hard line.

The look he was starting to hate. "What can I possibly do that would please you?"

The baby spit out the bottle, and Josie dipped her chin

to focus on him. Her hair swung forward, hiding her eyes from him. "Never mind. You can only do what you can do."

It was true. Hadn't he realized that himself? Hadn't he resigned himself to it when he'd finally left Texas and moved here to get a fresh start?

Josie murmured to the baby, communicating in sounds more than words, as if she'd forgotten Reed was even there. Eyes soft, she made shapes with her mouth, rounding her lips in an O, then smoothing them into a wide smile.

Troy watched her as if she were the most fascinating thing in the world. He moved his own mouth, as if to echo.

The empty ache spread upward to Reed's chest, making it hard to breathe. He didn't get it. He hardly knew Josie Dionne. He certainly had no reason to care how she saw him. Yet as much as he wanted to sweep her hard words and judgmental looks away, he couldn't. He wasn't sure why, but what she thought of him was important. A measure. Of what, he wasn't sure. He just knew he'd tasted enough failure in his life. He didn't want to fail again. "So what do you think I should be doing for him?"

She looked up, her hair falling back from her face and cupping around her jawline. "Are you serious?"

"Yes, I want to know."

"Well, you could start by holding him."

That seemed simple enough. Definitely something he could handle. "Okay. What else?"

The lines creasing her forehead seemed to soften just a little. "You could try feeding him a bottle once in a while."

He nodded slowly. He'd watched Josie and Missy

feed Troy. It didn't seem too tough to figure out. "I can do that. Piece of cake. What else?"

The corners of her lips curled upward, not exactly a smile, but not a frown, either. "Okay, hotshot. You can change his diapers."

"Now, that might be taking this a little too far."

The curve to her lips flattened into a hard line.

He held up his hands. "Kidding. I'll try. I'll learn. I'll give it my all. By the time we find Honey, I'll be an old pro." And ready to fill the role of favorite uncle, provided the paternity test came back the way he hoped. The way it had to.

BY THE TIME REED and Josie arrived at the lab, she was feeling rather embarrassed about her tirade back at his apartment. She'd let emotion get the better of her. Taken out her frustrations on a man she'd just met. He didn't have to have the same desires as she did. She knew it took all kinds to make the world go 'round, kumbaya, and all that crap. She went to UC Berkeley, for crying out loud. Live and let live.

Then why did his rejection of possible fatherhood bother her so deeply?

She knew the answer, even if she really didn't want to admit it. She liked him. More than she'd liked a guy in a long time. And not only did her blood feel alive whenever she was around him, he could potentially give her everything she wanted. If only he wanted the same thing.

But he didn't.

And instead of accepting that and focusing on doing her job, she'd lashed out at him. For a woman who prided herself on being in control of her life, she really needed to get a grip.

After her friend Simon swabbed the inside of Reed's and the baby's cheeks, and Reed signed a form allowing the lab to release the test results to only him or Josie, they made their way to the hospital. When Josie saw Missy sitting up in her bed like a queen with bandages for a crown, tears blurred her vision.

"Oh, sweetie." Missy held out her arms, and Josie let her aunt engulf her in a giant hug.

When their embrace ended, Josie pulled back and looked Missy over. "How are you doing?"

"Oh, you know." Missy waved the question away and looked past Josie to where Reed stood holding the baby carrier. "So the two of you met. That's good. I've been trying to make that happen for a long time."

Josie bit the inside of her bottom lip. The last thing she wanted to do was blurt out something about Missy's matchmaking. She still wasn't happy about it. Maybe even less happy than before her aunt was attacked. But after almost losing Missy, she wasn't going to spend their first moments together being angry. Certainly not because of a man who didn't want to be a father.

Reed stepped closer and took Missy's hand like a doctor with a well-developed bedside manner. "I hope you got my message."

"I did. And it's totally unnecessary."

"Maybe, maybe not. But it's taken care of all the same."

Josie looked from her aunt to Reed. "What are you talking about?"

Reed shook his head. "Not important. Josie is helping me find Honey and the man who attacked you, Missy.

You don't have anything more to worry about, so just focus on getting better."

Josie recognized a brush-off when she heard it. And she wasn't about to let Reed steal control of the conversation so easily. She looked to her aunt. "What kind of a message did he leave for you?"

"Josie is also helping me with Troy."

Missy's face morphed into a wide smile. "How is the baby?"

"He's great." Reed set the baby carrier on the floor and unbuckled the infant. "Do you want to hold him?"

"I'd love to—you know that." Missy reached out, and Reed put him in her arms. She settled herself against the raised back of the hospital bed.

Josie blew out a stream of air. There was no competing with the baby for attention. Not where her aunt was concerned. The woman lived for babies. Sometimes Josie felt like she had more in common with her aunt than anyone in her family.

"Oh, thank you for bringing him to see me. He's the best medicine I could ever get. I'm so glad you kept that man from taking him."

Josie leaned forward. "You remember what happened?"

The joy on her aunt's face faded. "Of course. Every minute." She shook her head with a little shudder. "A horrible man."

"What do you remember?"

"He had blond hair and the meanest eyes I've ever seen. He walked into the boat like he belonged there. And when I asked him what he thought he was doing, he told me to shut my mouth."

Josie nodded, trying to encourage the memory. If Missy had had that much contact with the man, she might be able to give a better description than either she or Reed. "Have the police been here to talk to you?"

"No."

A weight settled into the pit of Josie's stomach. That was just what she'd feared. Too many cases and too few leads had pushed what the police suspected might be an interrupted burglary to the bottom of their priority list. "I'll make some phone calls to people I worked with." Whether they would do any good was another matter. It was hard to fight against the effects of budget constraints.

"Tell them to hurry if they plan on visiting me here. I don't plan to stay long."

"Mom said you're planning to stay with her and Dad when you get out of the hospital, right?"

Missy grimaced. "She badgered me into it."

"Aunt Missy, you can't stay alone. Not until we find out who that man was."

"You're right. You're right." She smiled down at Troy before returning her attention to Josie. "But he wasn't after me."

"You don't know that. I know the police think he was a burglar, but I just don't buy that."

"Oh, he wasn't a burglar."

"How do you know?" Reed asked.

"He told me himself. He said he wanted the baby."

"He said that?"

"Yes. He said he worked for the baby's father. That he was hired to bring the baby home."

Josie glanced at Reed, but instead of the glee she

expected to see on his face, his brows tilted low. "Did he say who the father was?"

"No."

"Did he say how he knew this was the baby he was looking for?"

"He didn't explain any of it. And when I told him he couldn't take the little sweetheart, he hit me. That's all I remember." She glanced from Josie to Reed and back again. "What kind of a father would hire someone like that?"

"I don't know." But she knew of one way they could find out. "We need to find Honey."

"I think he was lying. That whoever hired him isn't this little precious one's father at all."

"Why do you say that?" Josie asked.

"Because a baby this beautiful wouldn't have a father who would hire someone like that. He'd have a daddy like Reed. Kind. Generous. And so handsome. Don't you think, Josie?"

Josie did her best not to roll her eyes. So Missy was back on her matchmaking kick. Josie had no idea how she'd thought a blow to the head would stop her. "Missy…"

"It's true. He's even promised to pay my medical bills, did you know that?" She reached for Reed's hand. "I know you didn't want me to tell, but it's just such a relief to me. I thought Josie should know."

BOBBY STOPPED IN FRONT of some fancy-ass department store and gazed at a mannequin in the window. An eye-numbing pink dress covered the white plastic body and one of the hands held a purse big enough to hold a good-sized weapon. Not that he was interested in fashion. Not even the kind that seemed practical. No, he was only pretending to look while he kept his eyes glued to the reflection of the man, woman and baby across the street.

Especially that baby. The cash that kid would bring him could buy a lot of fancy dresses for a lot of fancy women, women who would be a lot more interested in him once they saw how fat his wallet had become.

Learning where Reed Tanner lived and picking up his trail had been easy. Having the patience to follow him and the top-heavy chick and not just blow their brains out and take the kid required a little more effort.

He'd had plenty of opportunities.

The two had been distracted, more wrapped up in avoiding each other's eyes than in what was happening around them. Walk up behind them, put two slugs in the back of their skulls, pick up the baby and he'd be home free. Only the possibility of a bigger payday had made him bide his time.

It might be a guess, but if an old girlfriend had dumped a kid in *his* boat, Bobby would be looking for her. And although he wasn't sure how the busty blonde fit into the picture, he would bet Tanner was doing the same thing. Patience. That was what he needed. And soon he would have the payday he deserved.

Chapter Six

By the time they had flashed Honey's photo to a dozen desk clerks in half a dozen hotels, Reed's feet hurt and Troy felt as if he weighed eighty pounds. Thankfully, Josie hadn't said anything about him offering to pay Missy's bills. He had asked the older woman to keep it quiet. And he'd thought she understood. But if there was one thing he'd discovered about Missy, it was that she did her own thing, for her own reasons. And she always seemed to be one step ahead of him.

So far, her niece seemed to have the same talent.

He turned his face into the brisk wind, hoping it would invigorate him into gaining a second wind of his own. "Maybe there are so many people that come through these hotels that Honey was just lost in the shuffle."

"Impossible. I doubt she's the type of girl people would forget."

Probably true. He had to admit that when they were together, he'd enjoyed the envious looks he'd gotten from other men. But somehow he thought of Josie as being more memorable than Honey. Josie was a force. Like her aunt, but petite and cute and built like…

"Might she have stayed someplace smaller? A bed and breakfast? One of those little boutique hotels?"

He shook his head. "If Honey liked anything about San Francisco and about Dallas, it was the size. She liked to say it made her feel she was destined for greater things."

Josie nodded. "And a bigger hotel would be easier to get lost in, if she was trying to stay invisible."

He'd believed Honey was in trouble from the moment he'd seen the note she'd left. But hearing what Missy's attacker had told her had brought that home. "Maybe she didn't stay anywhere. Maybe she knew this guy was after her baby. Maybe she was in a hurry."

"You mean she went straight to your boat from the airport? I suppose that's possible. And in that case, she's likely not in San Francisco anymore."

Good point. Would she fly back to Dallas? Or somewhere else? Truth was, he didn't know Honey as well as he'd assumed. Except for Jimmy, he didn't know her friends. Except for Tiffany, he didn't know her enemies. He didn't know where she came from, and he damn well didn't know where she was going. He didn't know much about her at all.

He tilted his head back, looking up at the sky, and imagined her in a plane flying to who knew where. His gaze landed on great arched windows towering over the city. A hotel that looked like a giant jukebox. "I remember an argument we had about that place."

Josie nodded, as if encouraging him to continue.

"Honey heard it had a bar on the top floor. She wanted to check it out. She said she couldn't wait to sip her wine and look down on the rest of the city."

"And did you go?"

"No." He'd ignored her request. Thought it was silly. He'd been more eager to visit the smaller, more quirky side of the city, and he'd enlisted his friend to help get his way.

Josie craned her neck backward and stared up at the tower. "I think we've found Honey."

It didn't take long for them to cover the four blocks to the San Francisco Marriott. The muscles in his shoulders felt stiff, tight, and he doubted it all had to do with carrying the baby up and down the San Francisco hills. Even though they'd finally found a direction, he felt uneasy. Like they were running out of time.

As soon as the woman in front of them dragged her wheeled luggage out of the way, Reed stepped to the desk. "I'm looking for a woman I believe is staying here. Her name is Honey Dawson."

"Honey Dawson," the clerk repeated in a voice that was a little too cheery to jibe with Reed's mood. She punched in the name, then frowned at the screen. "It looks like you're too late. She checked out this morning."

They'd missed her.

Josie stepped to the counter alongside him. "We have some papers we were supposed to deliver to her, and I'm afraid we're late. Did she leave a forwarding address? Someplace we can mail them?"

"I'm afraid we don't give out that kind of information."

"She's going to be in big trouble if she doesn't get these papers. Can you tell me if her flight has left? Did she call for a cab?"

The woman pursed her lips and shook her head.

Great. Now what? He looked to Josie. Hopefully she had some ideas.

She smiled at the woman, obviously controlling any

impatience more effectively than he was. "Might the concierge be able to tell us more?"

"She might have taken a shuttle."

Reed snapped his attention back to the desk clerk. Now they might be getting somewhere. "Thank you. Do you remember what company?"

"I didn't say she *did* take a shuttle. Just that she *might* have. A lot of our guests find them convenient."

Reed tried to keep a cap on his impatience. "What company?"

"There's only one that serves our hotel."

"Thanks so much." Josie shot Reed a glance and started for the lobby door. Beyond the glass, a family unloaded from a shuttle van.

Reed adjusted his grip on the baby carrier and moved to follow.

"Wait."

The voice was so soft, Reed wasn't sure he heard it at first.

"You must be careful."

He turned to see a small woman with mousy blond hair. She was dressed in the white button-down shirt and black pants a hotel worker might wear, yet the clothing was wrinkled and one of the blouse's sleeves was torn. "Excuse me?"

"You must be careful," the woman repeated, some kind of Eastern European accent flavoring her words. "You must go away from here. You must hide him."

There were crazies in every city, and San Francisco had its share. He smiled at the woman and shook his head.

"Miss Dawson, she gave yo—"

"You know Honey?"

She nodded and motioned him closer.

Reed glanced back for Josie.

She'd reached the hotel door and was trying to flag down the shuttle driver.

Reed turned back to the mousy woman. "A man with short, blond hair?"

A small tremor moved through the woman's body. She straightened her spine and thrust out her chin. "He was here two times."

"Looking for Honey?"

"The first time, I lied. To protect the baby. The second time, he did this." She pulled the collar of her blouse a few inches to the side. An inflamed welt marred white skin.

A cigarette burn. Reed's stomach turned. "He did that to you?"

"He was very angry that I lied. That I told Miss Dawson to go, to run."

"You told her to run? Where?"

"I don't know where. Just away from here." She covered the wound, flinching as the cotton hit her skin. "You must hide the baby. You can't let him see."

"Who does he work for?"

She shook her head. "Go. If he sees you…"

"If he sees me, what? What does he want with the baby?"

Her gaze darted around the lobby as if she was sure the man who'd burned her was here, closing in.

All Reed saw were a few businessmen and a family of tourists. No blond hair. No gray coat. Nothing for this woman to be afraid of. Was she for real? "How do you know Honey Dawson?"

"I babysit."

"You took care of her baby? *This* baby?"

She glanced down at the baby bucket where Troy had thrown back the blanket and was waving his arms in the air. "Not that baby."

Now he was really confused. And beginning to think she was giving him some kind of runaround. Maybe trying to con him out of his money. How, he hadn't figured out. "What baby did you care for?"

"The baby I stayed with was a girl."

"A girl? That couldn't have been Honey Dawson. You must be mistaken."

"No mistake. I stayed with the girl. She took the boy with her."

The girl? Could this be for real? He leaned forward, his palm slick on the baby carrier's handle. "She had two babies?"

"Two babies, yes. This one and his twin sister."

JOSIE STEPPED BACK into the hotel and out of the light drizzle that had begun to fall. When she'd raced out of the lobby to catch the shuttle driver, Reed had been right behind her. Or so she'd thought. She had no idea how she'd lost him. For crying out loud. Next time she'd have to hold his hand and pull him along with her.

She firmly pushed that idea from her mind and scanned the lobby for the man she was beginning to think of as Captain Mess With Josie's Mind. She still didn't know what to think of his promise to Missy. And the actual attempts he'd made so far toward taking care of the baby, even if they hadn't gone much beyond holding him, had only made her more confused. It was sad. She was a grown woman with her own business, what there was of it, and she felt like a teen with a crush. Even when he acted like the commitment-phobic playboy she knew him to be, she couldn't help being attracted to him.

Like now.

He stood near the corner of the lounge, talking to a woman with more interest than Josie ever remembered a man showing her.

She stepped around a man with cropped dark hair and made her way back across the marble floor. At least she would get the baby. If he needed a few more minutes to get a phone number, so be it. It was a good reminder of how bad he was for her.

He spotted her before she was halfway across the lobby. Stepping out from the corner where he and the woman were huddled, he waved Josie over, the move abrupt with urgency.

Maybe she'd judged the situation a little too quickly. She scampered to his side. "Did you find something?"

"She babysat for Honey."

She glanced at the woman he'd been talking to, then back to Reed, trying to make sense of what he was saying. "She took care of Troy?"

"Not Troy." He looked at Josie pointedly, as if preparing for some kind of punch line. "Troy's twin sister."

She couldn't have been more shocked if he'd told her Troy was her very own child. "Twins?"

"Come here." He turned around and froze in his tracks.

The woman he'd been talking to, the one Josie had just seen, was now gone.

Reed grabbed up the baby's seat in one hand and caught Josie's hand in the other. He strode toward the hotel's far door, pulling her along. "I don't know if something or someone spooked her or what, but I don't think we want to take the chance."

"What's going on?"

"We'll talk about it outside."

She quickened her pace to keep up, while scrutinizing the handful of faces in the hotel lobby. Could he be right? Could Honey have had twins? And if she did, why leave only one in Reed's boat? Where was the other?

Reed pushed through a revolving door and careened out into a covered circular drive. The place was empty other than a doorman and a couple of smokers tending to their addiction. No cabs. With the drizzle they were probably plenty busy and didn't have to wait outside a hotel for fares.

"This way."

She followed Reed past the smokers and out onto the street. The sidewalk glistened under the cloudy sky. People rushed past, heads bowed. A few carried umbrellas.

"Wait." Josie reached down to the baby's carrier and flipped the visor up to shield him from the elements. They continued, blending with the other pedestrians hurrying down the street.

Reed swerved into a pedestrian mall midblock. Halfway up, he ducked into the sheltered doorway of a restaurant. The tangy sweetness of curry swirled in the air around them.

After a quick check on the baby, Josie faced Reed. "Okay, what's going on? Twins? What did she tell you?"

Reed didn't meet her gaze. Instead he kept watch on the empty concrete mall through squinted eyes. "Honey hired her to babysit yesterday morning. She stayed with the girl while Honey took Troy with her."

"To your boat?"

"It had to be. The timing is right. I arrived around dawn, and the baby was already there."

"And then?" He'd said there was more. More than the fact that Honey had twins. And whatever that more was, she had the feeling it was behind their escape onto the rainy street.

"She said a man showed up at the room looking for Honey."

A man? The image of Missy's attacker lodged in her mind. "What did he look like?"

"It was our guy. Short blond hair. Long coat."

"Did he tell her what he wanted?"

"Just that he was looking for Honey. And he asked about the babies. Whether Honey had them with her or left them in the hotel room."

"She didn't tell him…?"

"No. She told him Honey had taken the babies with her. She told him there had been a plumbing problem, and she was cleaning the room. But he came back."

Josie looked over her shoulder, half expecting a broad-shouldered man with short blond hair to be hulking behind her. "When?"

"After Honey had returned and gone. A little after sunrise."

"Without Troy?" She'd asked the question, but she already knew the answer. Honey had left the little boy on Reed's boat.

"She came back for the little girl. The maid told her our guy was there. That's when Honey left for the airport."

So that was it. They'd missed Honey. Unless the man who'd attacked Missy caught up to her, Honey had boarded a jet and flown who knew where. "Does she know where Honey went?"

"No. All she knew was that she took the shuttle to the air—"

She followed Reed's stare down the open expanse of wet concrete. A man strode quickly down the edge, his shoulders slumped forward, his gray coat pulled tight, dark head bowed.

The man she'd noticed at the hotel. A man with short dark hair. "Reed?"

He snapped his eyes to her. "I think that's him. I think that's the man who attacked Missy."

"You sure?"

"I think he dyed his hair." Reed cursed under his breath.

Josie slipped her hand into the bag. She fitted the pistol's grip into her palm.

The man stopped and pulled open a glass door. If Josie was judging the distance correctly, it had to be the back door leading into the hotel. The glass door closed behind him.

Once again gripping the baby's carrier and Josie's hand, Reed pushed out of the restaurant. "Go, go, go."

Leaving the gun in her bag, Josie scampered to keep up. There was a chance she was wrong, that the man they'd just seen duck into the hotel wasn't the same one at the boat yesterday. But she wasn't going to wait around to find out, and she doubted Reed would want to, either.

They reached Market Street. Two cabs passed, filled with passengers. Josie glanced back over her shoulder. The wet sidewalks were clear, but that didn't make her feel any better. "Chinatown."

Reed glanced at her, then tried to hail another cab to no avail.

"Tons of shops, probably people, what better place to get lost? We can't stay here. And it seems every cab in the city is taken."

"Okay." At the change of the light, Reed started across the street.

Josie hurried to keep up with his long stride. She hoped they were overreacting, that the man she'd spotted was no more than a businessman returning to the hotel to pick up something he'd forgotten. But as much as she wanted that to be true, she had a feeling it wasn't.

They scurried the few blocks up Grant Street. The gateway to Chinatown loomed over them. A man stood in the rain snapping a picture of a woman posing in front of the landmark, the yellow umbrella over her head making her face appear sallow.

Craning her neck, Josie peered over her shoulder at the slope they'd just climbed.

A man in a gray coat strode up the hill, two blocks behind.

"Reed." She ducked into a gift shop, Reed right behind her. Her bag swung heavily against her hip, the pistol inside. If worse came to worst, she could protect them. If he was unarmed, she could stop the man no matter how strapping his shoulders, no matter how muscular his arms.

But if he had a gun?

She pushed the image from her mind. They needed to lose him. She couldn't let it come down to some kind of shoot-out in the middle of a populated street. They had to get away.

They threaded through narrow aisles crowded with

displays of everything from silk kimonos to paper fans to small plastic toys. The scent of spicy perfume clogged in Josie's throat. Rounding a glass case filled with pearls, she spotted a back exit. She grabbed Reed's sleeve. He nodded, and they ran for the sign. Once they were outside, they'd be home free. There was no way the guy could guess where they'd gone. There was no way he'd catch up to them then.

"You not go there." A sharp voice rang out from across the store.

They kept moving.

"Employees. Just employees. You can't go."

They reached the end of the glass cases and flanked a pile of tea pots shaped like dragons.

"Stop."

Reed pushed through the silk curtain with one hand, holding the carrier behind him in the other. Josie followed him into a narrow hall that spilled into a room jumbled with boxes.

"Where's the door?" The panicked note made her own voice unrecognizable, even to her.

"It's got to be here somewhere." Reed moved through the boxes, then turned back.

Josie scanned the shabby white walls. "There has to be a fire exit, doesn't there?" But even though she asked, she knew there wasn't one.

Their luck had just run out.

Chapter Seven

The curtain over the door flapped open. An older man stormed into the storeroom. Face red, he flailed his arms in the direction of the store's front door. "Get out of here. Out!"

"Is there a back exit?" Josie asked. They couldn't go back out on the street. The man would be closer by the time they reached the front entrance. Maybe even on the same block. He'd see them for sure.

"No, no exit."

"What if there's a fire?"

"No, no fire. Now go out. Go out. This for employees only." He made a sweeping motion with his hands.

They moved back into the store. Josie watched the door. If Mr. Crewcut had made note of what store they'd gone into, they were in trouble.

"What kind of a place can get away with having no fire exit?" Reed squinted toward the front of the store. Josie was about to make a comment when he held a finger to his lips.

She followed his gaze to the open front door. A man with dark, short hair and broad shoulders stepped inside.

Her heart lurched against her ribs. So much for sneaking out the front door. With the man now inside the shop, they only had a moment before he'd see them. They had to find a place to hide, and they had to do it now.

She scanned the store, focusing on a circular rack jammed with embroidered silk robes. The kind of rack her niece and nephew loved to play in.

She grasped Reed's arm and motioned to the rack. *Over there. In the center.* She mouthed the words, praying he'd understand.

Reed nodded.

Keeping low, Josie moved quickly toward the clothing. Splitting her way between the garments, she slipped into the vacant space inside. Reed passed the baby seat to her, then scrunched in behind her.

As cool as it had been outside in the rain, with their bodies so close and the silk all around them, the heat was tropical in here. Reed's breath whispered against her cheek. Her pulse thrummed in her ears.

Footfalls vibrated along the floor beneath her feet. Whether the steps were advancing or fading, she couldn't tell. A creaking sound filtered up from deep in the folds of silk.

The baby. He was awake.

Please little guy. Don't cry. Don't cry.

She bent her index finger and offered him her knuckle. He clamped on, his tongue cupping around her finger. The hard edge of his emerging tooth pressed against her skin.

Thunk. Thunk. Thunk.

The footfalls were closer now. She could feel it. Not in

the vibrations, but in the way the oxygen had gotten thin. The way pressure assaulted her chest, too tight to breathe.

Voices shuffled in the air outside their cocoon. The store owner mumbled something under his heavy accent, too faint to hear.

A grunt came from somewhere else. "You sure?"

"They go."

The vibrations on the floorboards started again. Going away? Josie thought so, but she couldn't be sure, and she didn't dare peek her head up to look.

Time passed; how long, she wasn't sure. The baby sucked at her knuckle. She could feel the thump of Reed's heart in her chest, indistinguishable from the beat of her own.

"You leave my store now." The store owner's voice spoke loudly from above them.

Josie looked up to see his bland face peering down at them. "Is he gone?" she asked.

"Yes."

Reed moved the silk aside and peered out of the clothing rack. "It's clear." He climbed out from between the clothing and reached back for the baby seat.

Josie pulled her finger from Troy's mouth and handed the seat to Reed, then fought her way free of the silk. The baby squawked his protests.

Reed turned to the shop owner. "Call 911."

The man waved his hands in the air. "No. No police."

Josie wasn't surprised, but that didn't mean she was eager to step outside the shop without a police escort. "That man is dangerous. He might be waiting for us."

"Your problem. No police. Asking questions. Stopping business. No police." He glanced in the direction of the back room.

Josie dipped her hand into her bag and pulled out her cell phone. Maybe the shop owner didn't want to call 911, but she would. She flipped open the phone.

The shop owner lunged for her. "No. Please. I will show you a way out."

"There's another way? Why didn't you tell us that before?"

The man stared at her as if he had no idea what she'd just asked.

Reed grasped her shoulder. "It's fine. It's fine. We'll call once we're outside."

She clapped the phone shut.

Reed turned back to the owner. "We are grateful for your help. Show us the other way."

They followed the man in the direction of the front entrance. In a corner, just inside the outer door, a small hall jutted off to the side and led up a narrow staircase. The man led them up the steps, through the second-floor residence and down a fire escape into a side alley.

After passing along their thanks, Reed motioned for Josie to follow. Once outside, they headed up the hill. She made her 911 call, asking for a squad to be sent as they moved deeper into Chinatown.

The wind hit cold. Josie flipped up the visor and snuggled the baby's blanket tighter around him. He was full-out whining now, his hunger ramping up right on schedule. But as bad as she felt for him, they didn't have time to stop for a bottle any more than they dared stop and wait for the police. Not until they could get somewhere safe.

She blinked against the needle pricks of rain on her cheeks. Surely there was an empty taxi somewhere in this town. But until they found one, they would get lost among the checkerboard of streets running up and down and across the steep slope. They would get lost amid the jumbles of shops and restaurants.

They covered two blocks. Three. Her thighs burned with the climb. She squinted into the wet wind, checking to make sure Troy was still bundled tight. She loved San Francisco weather. It was never hot. Always invigorating. But when it rained, especially a cold, windy rain like this, she doubted there was anyplace more unpleasant in the world.

A flash of yellow car caught her eye on the street ahead. The dark silhouette of the driver hulked behind the wheel. The rest of the vehicle looked vacant.

"Taxi!" She threw her hand in the air and vaulted into the street. She waved, frantic, edging as close to the meager stream of traffic as she dared. "Taxi!"

The car swooshed past them and flowed down the hill. She turned her head to watch it go and looked straight into the eyes of a man standing twenty feet away, next to a family of tourists…the man who'd attacked Missy.

JOSIE REACHED INTO HER handbag.

Reed followed her line of sight and saw him. Damn. The guy's leg was cocked, his weight balanced on one cowboy-boot heel as if ready to spring forward. His arm hovered at his side. He held something in his fist. His gaze flicked away from Josie and focused on Reed. No. Lower. On the baby carrier in Reed's hand.

"Take the baby. Get out of here. I can hold him off."

Josie pulled her hand from her bag. A lethal-looking gun filled her palm. She wrapped her second hand around her first, arms straight in front of her, barrel pointing to the ground.

What did she think she was going to do? Make a last stand? "We'll all go."

"I can hold him off."

"And hit innocent bystanders? Or get hit yourself?" He'd only just met this woman, but the thought of her hit by a bullet, hurt, or killed… "We can't sit around and wait."

"I'm trained to use the gun. I can—"

"You can't stay behind." Reed sprang off the curb. Grabbing Josie's sleeve, he pulled her with him. She stumbled backward, holding the gun low in front of her. The people around them erupted in gasps, staring at the weapon.

Where the hell were the cops?

A car's tires screeched. A horn blared. They reached the other side of the street before the man moved.

"Run." Reed tightened his grip on Josie's hand. She spun and ran beside him. They rounded the corner of a building.

A siren cut the air. Still too far away.

"Go. I'll keep him here until the police arrive."

The rumble of a cable car niggled at his ear. He turned to see the Powell-Mason line trundling up the hill toward them. "We'll jump on the cable car. Put some distance between us."

She looked back toward the corner of the buildings.

She wasn't listening. He could tell. "You can't stay behind. You can't stay. I need you."

Her eyes flicked back to him.

"I don't know if I can jump on while holding the baby. Not without hurting him."

Her chest rose, drawing in a shaky breath.

"Here it comes."

She slipped the gun back into her purse.

If they did manage to board, would the car move fast enough to get away? Would the cops reach them in time to deter the pursuer? Reed wasn't sure. He saw the gray coat round the corner just as the cable car crested the hill. "Run."

Josie took off, running easily along the tracks. He followed, trying to keep the baby seat steady. The little guy flailed his arms, his complaints turning to all-out crying.

There would be time to comfort him once they put some distance behind them. Right now, all Reed could do was pray they'd make it. That the cops would arrive. That the gripman wouldn't stop the car and toss them off. That the man behind them was as reluctant to start gunplay in the streets as they were. Anything.

The cable car moved past him and caught up to Josie. She grasped one of the brass bars and leaped onto the steps. Twining a leg around the bar, she reached toward him.

Gritting his teeth, he hefted the baby seat to her hands. He had to run faster. Had to keep up. Pushing his legs to move, he reached her hands. Her fingers closed around the handle, and the weight lifted from his arms. An older woman helped her bring the baby safely on board. Others stared, not moving from their spots.

Now it was his turn.

Josie pointed past him. She shouted something, something he couldn't make out.

He tensed, waiting for the sound of a shot, the force of a bullet to slam him from behind, waiting for the strength to go out of his legs and leave him lying in the street.

The shot never came. He leaped for the cable car. His hand grasped cold brass. His foot found purchase. He pulled himself onto the car next to Josie and the baby just as the car crested the hill and started its plummet down to the bay.

WHEN THE DETECTIVE Reed had talked to the previous day heard about their newest brush with the man in the gray coat, his attitude was very different. After responding to Reed's call, Detective Martinez had picked the three of them up from Reed's apartment and had driven them to the precinct headquarters. Now they sat in a small conference room that smelled of body odor and furniture wax and waited for Martinez to return and provide them with a chance to flick through mug shots in an effort to identify the man who'd chased them through Chinatown.

Reed held Troy against his shoulder the way Josie had shown him and patted the baby's back. Holding him felt awkward, as if his hands were way too big and clumsy. But he was doing it, and the baby wasn't crying or complaining or thrashing around. In fact, if Reed had to guess, he'd say Troy was falling asleep.

"Do you want me to take him? I can set him in his infant seat so you have your hands free."

Unsure if he could master that maneuver himself quite yet, Reed nodded. "Thanks."

Josie lifted him from Reed's shoulder and snuggled

him gently into his seat. The baby's head lolled to the side. "He's out."

Reed wanted to chuckle at the obviousness of the statement, but the laugh wouldn't come. "It's no wonder. He went through a lot."

"We did, too."

He couldn't argue there. He still hadn't absorbed all that had happened in the past two days. But he did know one thing. Everything had changed. And their close call in Chinatown had made it clear to him that he could no longer deny that fact. "I have to talk to you. Tell you something."

She glanced up from the baby.

Now that her attention was on him, all the eloquent words he'd planned to say fled from his mind. All he could focus on was the questioning slant to her brows, the guarded look in her eyes and what expectations might be behind both. He swallowed into a tight throat. "This morning you said something to me. You told me to be a man."

Josie settled back into her chair, a sheepish look on her face. "Listen, I'm sorry. I—"

"Don't be. It's true. I was acting like this situation was going to go away, resolve itself on its own. Or with the results of a test. Or by returning Troy to Honey." Pressure built behind his eyes.

He thrust himself from his chair and walked the length of the cramped room, buying time, space. He didn't know how to explain this to her, what he'd realized when he saw her with that gun, when he saw her put herself on the line, try to take control, even when there was no real control to be had.

"You don't have to say any more."

"Yes. I do." He forced his feet to carry him back to his chair, but he didn't sit. He couldn't relax. He wouldn't until this mess was truly over. "It's important to me that you understand."

"Okay."

Again he groped for the words and came up empty.

"Just blurt it out."

Blurt it out. He could do that, couldn't he? He pulled a deep breath into tight lungs. "I don't know if I'll be able to take care of Troy, to fix things for him. But I just want you to know I'm going to try. Whether he and his sister are mine or not, he is my responsibility now, and I'm going to do right by him." The whole spiel sounded stupid, canned, stiff. But it was all he could come up with. He just hoped she knew he meant it down to his bones.

She nodded slowly. The corners of her lips curved upward. "I'm glad. So where do you see us going from here?"

He didn't know. And that worried him. It was one thing to promise to do his best and quite another to actually succeed. He just hoped he didn't let Troy down...or Josie. "I've been trying to figure out where Honey might go next. Where she might take Troy's twin."

"And?"

"That's the problem. I don't know. She's from a small town in Dawson County, Georgia, but I don't know exactly where. And I don't think she had many ties there. Except for one girl she was friends with in foster care, she never talked like she had any good memories."

"You don't know the girl's name?"

He shook his head. Just another detail he didn't know about Honey's life. "I just keep coming back to Dallas."

"What about Dallas?"

It was a small detail, and it could easily be nothing, but right now he felt it was the best they had. "The man who was following us. Did you notice his shoes?"

Josie frowned, that tiny furrow digging in between her eyebrows. "His shoes?"

"Not shoes, actually. Boots. He was wearing cowboy boots. Now, I've yet to see anyone in San Francisco wearing boots like that except me."

"But people wear them all the time in Texas?"

He tilted his head to the side in a pseudoshrug. "It's more common, anyway."

"So you think he followed Honey from Dallas?"

"Seems to make sense. If he's from Dallas, maybe whoever hired him is from Dallas, too." The twins' father, if they could believe what the would-be kidnapper had told Missy. Although Reed wasn't sure what he believed anymore. "It also seems whoever this guy is might not expect us to go back to Dallas. Not if he's intent on looking for us here. And that increases the odds of keeping the baby safe."

"You're taking the baby?"

"And you, if you'll agree." He pulled in another breath and held it. If she turned him down, he didn't have a clue what he'd do. Committing to try to make things right for the baby and actually taking care of him day to day were two separate things. And in the past two days he'd come to rely on Josie for other things, too. The prospect of delving into Honey's past was an uncomfortable one. The idea of doing it without Josie's help seemed impossible. "I'll pay for the plane ticket, of course. And I have a place to stay when we get there."

She curled her lower lip inward and clamped it between her teeth. For a long time, she said nothing. She just stared at the baby.

"Will you?" Reed prodded.

She released her lips and raised her eyes to his. "I guess so. You have a lot to learn when it comes to caring for a baby, that's for sure. And I obviously don't know how to say no."

Chapter Eight

The plane jolted as it touched down on the Dallas/Fort Worth International Airport runway. Josie forced herself to yawn, her ears popping to equalize the pressure. Strapped into his chair in the seat beside her, Troy sucked ferociously on his pacifier. He'd been so good on the flight. Amazing what the little rubber nipple could do. Even the adjustment of pressure hadn't bothered him.

Of course, that wasn't what was bothering her, either. Nor was she tense about leaving San Francisco on such short notice. After their scare in Chinatown, flying a thousand miles away seemed like a good idea. No, the thing that had her stomach feeling like it was tied in a bow was the man sitting in the seat behind her on the 747.

She was grateful they hadn't been able to get seats together on such short notice. The flight had given her time. To think. To sort through all that had happened. Not that the few hours in the air had been enough.

The first time Missy had told her about Reed, she'd known exactly what kind of guy he was. A playboy. A forever bachelor. A man who avoided responsibility.

The kind of man she'd fallen for before, and the kind of man she knew she had to avoid at all costs. She'd gone through the roller-coaster ride men like that brought with them. And she knew she risked having her heart completely shredded.

But this last turn of events she wasn't sure how to interpret. A man who avoided responsibility wouldn't feel obligated to a baby, would he? Especially one he didn't know for certain belonged to him. That man wouldn't promise to help pay Missy's hospital bills. That man wouldn't put his life on hold and travel across the country because he was worried about an old girlfriend.

For a man who said he wanted to avoid responsibility, in the last few hours Reed Tanner had gone out of his way to take it on his shoulders. It didn't make sense.

Unless she had been wrong about him.

Her head felt light, dizzy with the new revelation. And what it meant. If he wasn't irresponsible, if he wasn't the playboy bachelor, if he wasn't everything she had learned to steer clear of, that made him all the more tempting. And that's what worried her most of all.

A squawk ripped from the seat next to her. Troy flailed his hands and complained about the loss of his pacifier.

She plucked the pacifier from where it sat on his belly, popped it back in his mouth and glanced at her watch. Sure enough. The little guy wanted his meal. His stomach was regular as clockwork. "We'll get you a bottle as soon as we get off the plane, okay? And if you play your cards right, a clean pair of pants, too."

He blinked those big eyes. His fat cheeks gathered upward in a smile.

A smile just for her.

A cramp settled deep in her chest. She dreaded more with each passing day the moment when she found Honey and reunited her with Troy. She hated to think what life would be like without seeing his smiles, smelling his sweet baby breath, listening to the little grunts he made while he slept. If she was worried about Reed stealing her heart, she was twice as worried about the child.

Who was she kidding? There was no point in worrying about that. Troy already owned her heart, and she would be devastated when she had to leave him.

She gathered the baby bag from under the seat as the plane taxied to the gate. There was only one thing she could do. Figure out who the man in San Francisco was and who hired him, find Honey, and get the hell back to San Francisco before she fell even deeper for this sweet baby…or the man who might be his daddy.

"IT'S NOT FANCY, that's for sure." Reed swung the rental car onto the gravel road and drove under the Double Kay Ranch sign. The tires vibrated over the cattle guard, making the whole car shake. Up ahead, the ranch looked as dismal and depressing as it had when he'd packed up and left. No, even more so. The pipe corral needed paint. The whitewashed barn was missing a few boards, the light of sunset glowing through spaces between the others. The old truck he'd left for dead had picked up a heap more rust. And without a single horse or head of cattle or barking dog on the ranch, the air outside was deathly quiet.

And too damn hot.

He hadn't realized how used to the San Francisco climate he'd become over the past year. But more than any September he could remember, the Dallas area felt like one big blazing oven.

He drove along the barbed-wire pasture fence and came to a stop in front of the boxy-looking ranch-style house. The paint had faded over the last year, changing to an even paler shade of blue. But other than that, the house hadn't changed a bit. Not the look of it, and not the oppressive feeling of failure that assaulted his chest the closer he came to stepping through its door.

Josie turned to face forward after checking on Troy in the back seat. She held a hand up to shield her eyes. "It might not be fancy, but it's kind of cute." The sun's orange glow warmed her skin and made her squinted eyes look as though they were twinkling.

"You're the one who's kind of cute."

She frowned and averted her eyes.

He knew he shouldn't have said it out loud, but it was true. She was mighty cute. And right now, he was very grateful she was with him. Facing the Double Kay, the town of Springton and the whole Dallas/Ft. Worth area with her by his side was a lot easier than doing it alone. Or with only the baby.

A brief stop at Honey's apartment had gotten them nowhere. She wasn't home. Hadn't been for days, according to a neighbor. Nothing Reed hadn't already figured out from his one-sided chat with Jimmy. After they'd left her apartment, Reed had thought a green pickup truck was following them, a little bit of paranoia that turned out to be a false alarm. But the thing he'd found most annoying about returning to Texas was the bland pop that radio stations were passing off as country music. He couldn't wait to get back to San Francisco and his collection of Dale Watson CDs.

Of course, he had the feeling these were only the first in a series of frustrations heading for him. He might as well get the next miserable experience out of the way as soon as possible. "Let's go inside."

Carrying the baby in his seat, Reed led Josie up the steps and opened the door for her. He ushered her in first and waited for her reaction.

The hard line of her mouth softened ever so slightly. "It's nice."

"Nice?" He glanced around at shabby furniture, outdated carpet and interior walls that needed paint almost as much as the outbuildings. "I don't know about nice."

"It is nice. Unpretentious. Functional. Feels like home."

A laugh broke from his lips. No, more like a guffaw.

She turned to look at him, one side of her mouth tilting upward in a half smile. "Are you laughing at me?"

"No, no. I'm in awe that anyone could call this place nice."

"It is nice."

He shook his head. "It's outdated and run-down. At least that's the reason my Realtor gave for not being able to sell it."

"I noticed the sign when we drove up. How long have you had it on the market?"

"I just put it on last month."

"You moved to California a year ago, right? Why did you wait so long to try to sell it?"

"A number of reasons."

"I can relate to that." She gave him an understanding smile.

A smile he'd like to snap a photo of and keep forever. But somehow he doubted she could really relate to anything about his reasons for selling or not selling this place. "What can you relate to?"

"This is where you grew up, right? When my parents sold the house I grew up in, I grieved for weeks. I still miss that place. A lot of good memories there."

He shook his head. If there was one thing he didn't share with the Double Kay, it was good memories. Even his mother hadn't had many good words to say about it, and it had been in better shape back then. Still, she'd told him many times how embarrassed she was to live in such a dump when he was growing up. "Nothing like that. I'd be glad to be done with this place. Trust me."

"Then why are you only starting to try to sell it now?"

"That would be because of me."

Josie whirled around.

Reed smiled as Esme slipped out of the kitchen. Now, she carried good memories for him. Just about the only ones he had of his childhood. "Oh, Esme, you know you earned it. You raised me, after all."

She flicked her hands in the air as if brushing away his words. "Your mother was a good woman. She had hard times. She tried to do the right thing. She just didn't always make good decisions."

The last person Reed wanted to talk about was his mother. He gestured to Josie. "Esme, this is Josie. She's the one helping me find Honey." He'd called Esme before they'd left for Dallas and filled her in on some of the reasons he was coming back.

Esme reached out a weathered hand. "You're the private investigator from San Francisco?"

Josie took the offered hand and shook. "It's nice to meet you. Do you live here?"

"I did. For a time. That is the real reason Reed didn't sell the ranch right away. He was being kind to me. Letting me live here while I looked for work." She smiled up at Reed. "I have found a good job now and a place to live, all because of Reed's generosity."

"Generosity is what you showed me." And his mother.

"Your mother gave me a good wage for the work I did. You gave out of the goodness of your heart."

Reed shook his head and shrugged. Truth was, he was embarrassed by Esme's gratitude and more than a little aware of Josie's gaze on him, trying to size him up.

"So who does the *niño* belong to?" Esme bent down and smiled at Troy.

"He's Honey's. She asked me to take care of him for a little while."

Esme ran her fingertips over the baby's fine hair. "He looks much like you when you were little, Reed."

Josie glanced at Reed, and he knew she was sizing up his reaction.

He nodded, his eyes glued to Esme. "I was that cute, huh?" Truth was, he was starting to get used to thinking of Troy…not as his child exactly, but as a nephew or something. As a part of his life.

And he wasn't quite sure if that was good or bad.

JOSIE SPREAD A BLANKET over the football field printed on the bottom of the Dallas Cowboys playpen and laid Troy down on his back for a morning nap. Reed had done a good job of picking up the list of baby supplies and groceries she'd given him, and with Esme's help she

had turned Reed's vacant ranch house into their tempo-
rary home. After calling her parents' house to make sure
Missy was doing okay her first day out of the hospital,
both she and Reed had collapsed into bed early last
night. But even though she'd gotten little sleep the past
few nights, she hadn't been able to quiet her mind. Her
head hummed with questions. Not just about Honey
and the man who'd attacked Missy, but other things, as
well. And last night as well as this morning, those other
things were all about Reed.

The more Josie learned about this man, the more her
picture of him changed. For a man who had pretty much
called himself a failure in connecting with people, he
sure believed in coming through for the women who had
touched his life. Honey, Missy and now Esme.

And all she'd observed since they'd reached the ranch
last night made her even more curious about his mother.

She stood and slipped from the room, ignoring Troy's
fussy complaints. At the door, she hesitated. She could
hear Esme busy in the kitchen and Reed reciting his cell-
phone number in case of emergency. The normalcy of
leaving the baby with a sitter—as if the two of them
were a real couple and Troy was their child—ached
through her chest.

She took a grip on her thoughts before they spiraled
out of control. She could want Reed to change until the
end of time, but that didn't mean it would happen. And
she knew herself. Knew that if she wanted it badly
enough, she might just start seeing what she wanted to
see, regardless of what reality showed her.

She pulled in a breath and forced her feet to carry her
down the short hall. She had to tread carefully around

Reed Tanner. And one way she could do that was by keeping her thoughts off Reed and focused on the questions she wanted to ask Honey's friend Jimmy.

JIMMY WAS NOTHING IF NOT reliable. Reed had said he and Honey had met for lunch at Bertha's Bar-B-Que every Tuesday, and even though it was a year later and Honey was nowhere to be found, there was Jimmy sitting in a booth along the wall chewing on a pulled-pork sandwich. He was dressed all in black, even down to his tie and shirt, but his slightly mussed, sandy hair made him look like the boy next door despite the clothes.

Josie kept her focus on Jimmy, though she directed her words to Reed. "Let me talk to him."

She could feel him nod. "You won't get an argument from me. I doubt he'd say more than two words to any question I asked him, and both of those words would be profane."

They told the woman at the hostess desk someone was waiting for them and started across the dining room, winding around tables covered in checkered cloths and set with big napkins and plastic, adult-size bibs.

Jimmy looked up from his sandwich. His sharp eyes narrowed. He scooted out of the booth and grabbed the check from the tabletop.

Josie dodged in front of him, trying to head him off. "Please, Mr. Bartow. Wait. We need to talk to you."

"I don't know who you are, but I'm not talking to Tanner." He zigged to the side, trying to avoid her. She countered, stopping him face-to-face.

Reed stepped up behind her. "Honey left San Francisco without ever seeing me, Jimmy. I think she's in trouble. We need your help. Honey needs your help."

Jimmy stared at Reed, and if Josie wasn't mistaken, his lip curled upward slightly, like a dog baring his teeth. "What makes you think you know anything about what Honey needs?"

"A man was after her," Josie said, bringing his attention back to her.

"A man? Who?"

"We don't know. But he had short blond hair, broad shoulders and a gun."

"A… You're lying."

"No lies." Reed held his hands up, palms out. "Honey had twins a few months ago, a boy and a girl."

"In June. How is that any…" Jimmy's eyes flared open. "You think those babies are yours, don't you?"

"I don't know."

"Well, they're not. No way."

"The timing is right, Mr. Bartow," Josie added.

Jimmy didn't even spare her a glance. This was all about Reed and the rivalry he obviously felt. Jimmy was staking out his territory. "She wasn't sleeping with just you."

"Who else was she sleeping with?" prompted Reed. "You?"

The flush to Jimmy's cheeks spoke louder than a shout.

Josie glanced up at Reed, trying to judge his reaction.

Although his cheeks seemed to pale ever so slightly, nothing else in his expression changed. "You didn't send Mr. Hired Gun to collect her, did you, Jimmy?"

Jimmy splayed a hand on his chest. "Me? Of course not."

Reed cocked an eyebrow, as if he didn't buy it for a second. "You're not trying to use those babies to get to Honey? Force her to be with you? Maybe get married?"

"I would never force Honey to do anything. I love Honey."

Even without knowing much about Jimmy and Honey, Josie could sense the direction Reed was going with this. And she played along. "To a lot of people, love justifies control."

"It's not like that. She's my friend. The only person in this miserable world I really care about. And who cares about me."

Josie shook her head slowly. "But maybe she doesn't care enough. Maybe she's not as committed to you as you are to her. Maybe she needs some help to see what's really important."

Jimmy glanced from Josie to Reed and back again. "I know what you're trying to do. It won't work. Honey is my friend."

"Whom you sleep with." Josie pressed on.

"One time. That was all." He focused a pointed glare on Reed. "She'd just had her heart shredded and needed to know someone cared."

"So this happened after Reed moved?"

"No." Jimmy's glare turned smug.

A muscle flexed along Reed's jaw, but he said nothing.

"When did this night together happen?" Josie asked.

"That's none of your damn business."

"Listen, our hired gun said he was working for the twins' father." Josie let her comment hang in the air for a moment. Often if someone felt guilty of something, they rushed to fill any silence, imagining the quiet meant the speaker was thinking condemning thoughts. But when Jimmy didn't bite, Josie continued. "Are you the twins' father, Jimmy?"

He shifted his feet on the tile floor. "He told you that? That the father hired him to hurt Honey?"

"Yes." She saw no point in getting caught in details. Not when using this information as a club might actually beat the truth out of Jimmy Bartow.

One side of Jimmy's mouth turned up in a smug smile. "You implied this guy was bad news. Did it ever occur to you that he might also be a liar?"

It had. But what he'd said to Missy was all they had to go on at the moment. Beggars couldn't be choosers, as the saying went. "So you're saying that you're the father of Honey's babies, but you didn't hire this guy to track her down? Even when you found out she was taking your children to see Reed?"

"I'm saying nothing. I don't know who the father is." His voice cracked. He stumbled back to his booth and lowered himself onto the vinyl seat.

Reed slid in opposite him, and Josie took the spot by his side, boxing him in.

He stared into his coffee cup, as if he'd forgotten they were there. Finally he brought his gaze back to Josie's. "I don't know why Honey went to see him. I have no idea what she saw in him in the first place."

Josie wanted to believe him. He seemed to care about Honey. No, he seemed in love with her, as he'd admitted. She'd bet the thought that those babies probably weren't his hurt him deeply. But she'd seen men show that kind of devotion only to turn it into something obsessive and ugly. A justification for possessing and controlling the women they swore they loved. When she'd been a cop, she'd dealt with plenty of men like that. And in the short time that had passed since she'd hung out her shingle, she'd had two potential clients who'd wanted her to keep a twenty-four-hour surveillance over their wives. She'd turned the jobs down.

Was Jimmy Bartow one of those men?

Maybe if she could needle him a little more, he would show his true colors. "Were there other men who could have fathered those babies, Jimmy? Men besides Reed?"

"What are you trying to say?"

"I know Honey had a hard childhood. She was abandoned, raised in foster care. A lot of women who go through experiences like that—"

"Honey wasn't like a lot of women."

"But she was hungry for love. For security," Josie said. Reed had told her that much.

He didn't answer, but judging from the way he shifted on the seat, she was right on target.

"You had to notice the jewelry she started wearing just before I left town," Reed said.

From Josie's angle, she could see Jimmy open and close his fists under the table.

Reed pressed on. "And the expensive clothes? You noticed, didn't you?"

"So? She likes clothes. She likes jewelry."

"I didn't give her those things," Reed said, "and I have a feeling you didn't, either."

"How can you be so sure about that? Honey deserves nice things."

"I'm sure because those things cost more money than a bailiff could shell out."

His hands balled into fists and stayed there. The tendons in his neck drew taut.

"Jimmy," Josie said.

He didn't take his eyes from Reed. He seemed on the edge of trying to shut Reed up with his fists. A fantasy Jimmy had likely nurtured for a long time.

"Someone gave her those things, Jimmy," she said. "Someone with cash. Enough cash to hire a man to fly to San Francisco. Enough cash to pay him to take her babies away. Enough cash to hurt her."

Jimmy's focus snapped to Josie.

It had been a hunch on her part, but judging from Jimmy's reaction to her theory, he believed it to be true. And he knew more about Honey's sugar daddy than he wanted to let on. "Who is he, Jimmy? Who else did Honey sleep with during that time?"

He looked down at the table. Raising a hand from his lap, he began tracing the edge of his butter knife.

"I'm not going to let it go until I find out," she warned.

"That's Honey's business. Honey's privacy."

"It's not going to be very private if I start asking all the people who knew her. Her neighbors. Her hairstylist. The girls she knew on the cheerleading squad."

"I promised her I wouldn't tell."

Reed leaned across the table toward him. "So she confided in you? About her sex life?"

Jimmy jutted out his chin. "She confided in me about everything."

"Then who is it?" Josie asked again. "Who's the father of her babies?"

"He gave her gifts, but he's not the father."

"How do you know?"

He looked away.

"You don't know at all, do you? It's just wishful thinking." Something Josie knew far too much about.

Jimmy stared down at the table. Raising a hand, he rubbed his forehead hard enough to remove skin. "He can't be the father. Poor Honey. If he's the father..."

Josie leaned toward him. "If he's the father, what?"

"It will be a mess, that's all."

"Why?"

"Because he's already married. Because he could make her life hell."

Now they were getting somewhere. "Who is it, Jimmy? Who gave her the gifts?"

"The judge."

Reed sat back in his booth with a thud.

She pulled her focus from Jimmy and searched Reed's face. "The judge? Judge who?"

He stared past her, as if lost in his own thoughts.

"Reed, tell me. Who is the judge?"

"Judge Teddy Wexler," Reed muttered. "The man who pretty much owns Springton and everyone in it."

Chapter Nine

Reed was grateful to get out of Bertha's and into the blazing sun, even though it had to be a hundred degrees in the shade. He'd known the meeting with Jimmy wasn't going to be pleasant. But he'd had no idea they'd actually learn something from the little bandy rooster. Of course, what they'd learned had only served to make clear the force they were up against.

"So are you going to tell me why this judge has both you and Jimmy freaking out?" Josie parked herself on the sidewalk in front of him and plopped her fists on her cute little hips.

"I'm not freaking out."

"Could have fooled me."

He let out a heavy breath. "You didn't grow up in Springton. You have no idea what a force the judge is in this town. Hell, in all of Dallas/Ft. Worth."

"He's that big a cheese, huh?"

He smiled. "Yeah. I guess."

"So he's wealthy."

"And powerful."

"So if those babies are his, and he wants them,

Honey doesn't stand a chance? That kind of rich and powerful?"

"That's the kind."

"But he's married. Wouldn't it be scandalous for him to suddenly father twins with a young thing like Honey?"

"Scandal didn't stop him before."

"He had another baby with a mistress?"

"Not a baby in the end. She had a miscarriage. But a big blowup of an affair."

"What happened?"

Springton gossip happened. The juiciest kind. "He dumped his wife and married the younger model."

"Before or after the miscarriage?"

"Before."

"So he wants kids, I take it."

"I don't know what he wants. He has one kid."

"Why don't we find him and ask him what he wants?"

"You're kidding."

"No, I'm not." She tilted her head to the side, as if trying to read his mind. "Don't tell me you're afraid of the judge."

The comment made him smile. He'd been afraid of Judge Wexler when he was in high school, and later, when he had the ranch and his mother's well-being to worry about. But those days were gone. After his mother's death, he was released from the burdens that had haunted her. And now that Esme had found employment, he couldn't care less what happened to the ranch. He stuck his thumbs in his belt and leaned back on his heels. "Darlin', I ain't been afraid of no one since I was a boy."

"You were afraid of a twelve-pound infant until pretty recently."

He let out a chuckle. It felt good to laugh, especially at a topic Josie wouldn't have been joking about only a couple of days before. "Fair enough. Except for that. Compared to poopy diapers, dealing with Judge Teddy Wexler is going to be a piece of cake."

They located the judge easily enough. He was lunching in his chambers in the county courthouse. Unfortunately, finding him and talking to him were two totally different things.

"I'm sorry. The judge is very busy. If you'd like to make an appointment, I might be able to help." The older woman gave them a patronizing smile. "Now what's the name?"

"Honey Dawson," Josie said.

The woman's smile fell from her shiny pink lips.

Reed did his best to check the laugh struggling to break free. "Too bad. We were hoping to talk to him here. I guess we'll have to make the drive out to the Wexler Ranch. I hate to bother Mrs. Wexler."

The woman held up a finger. "Why don't I check with the judge? Maybe he can adjust his schedule."

Reed nodded. "Maybe he can."

As soon as the woman walked from the room, Josie smiled up at him. "Damn, we make a good team."

Reed couldn't argue. He'd never seen himself as part of a team with anyone, not even during his backup quarterback stint with the Springton Stallions. But this wasn't high school. And Josie was put together far better than any football player he'd ever seen. "I'd like to see how good."

As his meaning dawned on her, her smile faded.

"Oh, come on. I'm not such a bad guy."

"Maybe not. But that's beside the point."

There she went again. Still, he should be happy her opinion of him had seemed to improve. Something he would surely screw up if he kept teasing her this way.

"The judge does have a few minutes to see you," the secretary said walking back into the room. She held up a finger. "Only a few, mind you. He has a very busy afternoon."

"I'm sure he does." On the way to the judge's chambers, they'd checked the docket for his courtroom. No business was going on, not a single hearing. Of course official business wasn't what the judge was necessarily best at.

They followed the woman through the small suite of offices. She stopped at an imposing door and rapped with her knuckles as she pushed it open and motioned them inside.

The judge sat at a mahogany desk. Surrounded by shades of gold and rich burgundy, he looked like a king sitting on his throne. No doubt, that was precisely the image he wanted to project.

As soon as Reed stepped through the door, the air closed in around him, heavy and lacking in oxygen. It was the same feeling he'd had as a kid the few times he'd been in the judge's presence, and suddenly he had the urge to walk with his head down, the posture he'd seen his mother adopt around people like the Wexlers. The posture of a whipped dog.

"Have a seat." The judge motioned to two leather wing chairs positioned in front of his desk.

Josie perched on the edge of one of the chairs. Keeping his chin up and back straight, Reed remained standing.

Except for the gray that now dominated his hair, Judge Teddy Wexler looked just as Reed remembered. Brash, cocky and powerful. Even the way he sat had a swagger. A cross between cowboy and executive. He peered over the top of his reading glasses. "You don't sit, son?"

"We have some questions to ask you."

"And you can't ask them while sitting?"

Reed didn't move. "Where is Honey Dawson?"

"Honey Dawson?" the judge parroted, as if he'd never heard the name. He narrowed his eyes on Reed. "I know you, don't I?"

"We know you were involved with Honey. We also know you sent a man to San Francisco to find her." He'd debated being this aggressive with the judge, wondering if polite questions would get him further. But in the end, he sensed that winning the judge's respect up front was the best way to approach him. And the only way to do that was to come out swinging. When it came down to it, aggression was all the judge really respected. "What is the man's name, and where is Honey now?"

"I don't know what man you're talking about. But it is true that I'm looking for Honey."

"Why? What do you want with Honey?"

"That's my business."

"It wouldn't have anything to do with the twins she gave birth to last summer, would it?"

The judge slipped off his reading glasses and leaned back in his chair.

"I'll take that as a yes. I also take it you are responsible for the man following Honey. A man who has been seen with a gun. A man who hit one woman over the head and put out a cigarette on another when she wouldn't tell him where Honey went."

"I don't know what you're babbling about."

"You need a better answer than that. The San Francisco police have a description of the man, and witnesses who saw him try to hurt one of the children." An exaggeration, admittedly, but he needed to shock the judge. Surprise him enough that he dropped his guard. "I'd say it's only a matter of time before they find this hit man…and the judge who hired him."

"You think *I* hired a hit man?"

Reed wasn't sure if the incredulous response was real or put on, but there was one way to find out. He pushed on. "The guy is from Dallas. He was looking for Honey, looking for her babies."

The judge leaned forward and tilted his head to the side, as if he was sure he hadn't heard Reed right. "You think I want to hurt Honey and her babies?"

"No, why would we think that?" Reed let sarcasm drip from each word. The thought that Honey had anything to do with this man made him want to puke.

"The only person I know who might want to hurt Honey is a man named Neil Kinney."

"The stalker?" Josie asked.

The judge tilted his head in Josie's direction. "He was released on probation about a month ago."

Reed could feel Josie focus a questioning look on him. He shook his head. "I've seen Kinney. That wasn't him in San Francisco."

"Maybe Mr. Kinney sent the man you're talking about. All I know is it wasn't me. I have no reason to want to hurt Honey."

Josie crossed her legs. "But you have reason to want to find her, don't you? Or should I say you have reason to find her babies?"

Leaning back in his chair, the judge gave a low chuckle. "You're right, young lady. But not for the reason you think."

An uncomfortable twinge bit down on the back of Reed's neck. The judge's sudden smugness wasn't a good sign. Not good at all. He had the urge to take that invitation to sit, just in case the judge was about to pull the rug out from under him.

"I remember how I know you. It's Tanner, right?"

Reed didn't answer.

"This is all some kind of wild misunderstanding, Tanner. I didn't hire anyone to run around San Francisco assaulting babysitters and waving a gun. But I am looking for Honey—" He held up a hand. "No, no, that's not exactly true. I don't give a stitch about Honey Dawson. It's the twins I'm looking for."

"You're their father?" Josie asked.

The judge spread out his hands, as if that was a given. "So you see, I have no reason to want to hurt them."

Reed blew a derisive breath through his nose. "I can think of a lot of reasons. Your wife. The scandal. Child-support payments for eighteen years. If you really are the twins' father, you have every reason to want Honey and those babies to disappear."

The judge thrust up from his chair and swaggered over to the credenza. He picked up a photo, rubbing his thumb around the frame's edge as he studied the image. An image Reed knew all too well. "Tell me, Tanner. Does your father keep this picture on his desk?"

Reed clenched his teeth. The judge was well aware that he didn't know his old man. That Reed's father had left long before that photo was taken. It was the big scandal in Springton at the time. A scandal his mother's subsequent drinking problem only made linger.

"I'll bet he does. You see, there's no prouder moment in a man's life than when his son excels." He turned the picture toward Josie, giving her a good look. "State champion in high school football. That's a big deal in this state. A big deal. And there's my boy, Teddy Jr. First-string quarterback for the state-champion team."

"Congratulations," Josie said dryly. "But I'm afraid I don't see what this has to do with Honey Dawson and her twins."

"It has everything to do with them."

Josie raised her brows.

He set down the photograph. Giving the frame one last caress, he strolled back to his desk, drawing out the moment like a stage actor. "A man lives for the success of his children. Their accomplishments are the realization of his dreams. The legacy he leaves behind. His taste of immortality. Stuff you can only understand if you have a child. Problem is, some children stop producing. I haven't had any of those moments for a long time."

"And you see Honey's twins as a chance to collect more trophies?" Josie prodded.

"I see *my* twins as a chance to collect more, darling. A boy and a girl? Not much better than that. And between my athleticism and Honey's looks, those babies have success written all over them. They'll give me a chance to collect a lot more. Makes you want to have two of your own, doesn't it, Tanner?"

Reed knew there was a chance the judge was Troy and his sister's father. That's why they'd come to see him. But hearing him brag about it as he had with the picture of the football team and the fact that Reed never knew his father… The whole thing made him want to puke. Or just punch the judge in the face. It had to be a lie.

Josie held up her hands, palms out. "Let me get this straight. So you believe the twins are yours. And you have people looking for Honey and the babies?"

"I never denied that."

Reed had heard enough. He wanted to take the guy out. Bloody his nose. Make him experience a little of the fear Honey must have tasted. The fear that drove her to fly all the way to San Francisco, to leave her child alone on his boat before sunrise. "Your man had a gun. He burned one woman and put another in the hospital."

The judge shook his head, as if sorely disappointed in Reed. "Not my man. My people are lawyers. They aren't trying to hurt anyone. And neither you nor the San Francisco police are going to be able to prove anything different. I want to find those children. I want to welcome them into my family. I want to bring them home where they belong."

"Do you think he's telling the truth?"

Reed gripped the steering wheel and merged with the traffic buzzing along the freeway. He didn't want to believe any of it. Not one word. The thought that Judge Teddy Wexler was Troy's father… He just couldn't see it. "I think he's full of it."

"Sure?"

"You think he's telling the truth?"

"I think if Troy and his twin sister are his, it means they aren't yours. It's what you wanted."

He squirmed in his seat. He could feel Josie's gaze boring into him, trying to read his emotions, his thoughts. Maybe if she figured it out, she could tell him. God knew he couldn't figure it out himself. "So you think the twins are his now?"

"The judge seems sure."

"Or at least that's what he's telling us."

"Why would he lie? If he did hire the guy in San Francisco to make the problem go away, it seems stupid to admit the problem is true. And if he actually wants to raise his babies—"

"They aren't his babies." He didn't know why he'd said it. He didn't even know he was going to, not until the words had already left his lips.

Josie's head snapped around. She opened her mouth, then shut it without a word.

"Troy doesn't look anything like him."

Tires hummed on pavement. Hot wind whistled through Josie's open window.

He wished she would say something. Anything. "You don't think he does, do you?"

"You don't want to know what I think."

He probably didn't. But he couldn't stand her silence for another second. Whether she was judging him or had already condemned him, he'd rather know than sit here in the dark. "Try me."

"I think this has little to do with Troy and his sister. I think when it comes down to imagining Honey sleeping with Teddy Wexler when she already had you…getting pregnant with his babies…your ego can't handle it."

Her judgment of him slammed into him like a kick upside the head. Was that it? Were his doubts all about an insult to his manhood? "I have to admit, the thought makes me a little sick. But that's not all about this that's rotten. The timing doesn't work out."

"The timing?"

"You guessed Troy is three months old, right? Add that to nine months, and she hadn't started with Wexler yet."

"She was still with you."

"Yes." He waited for the dizziness to assault him, the pressure to weigh him down, the tightness to grip his throat. But nothing happened. "The twins must be mine."

"If guessing a baby's age was a science. And if the world worked according to standard timetables."

"What?"

"We're only talking about a two- or at the most three-week time frame." Her voice dropped, lending more emphasis to each word. "You can twist that to prove whatever outcome you want."

He gripped the wheel and stared out at the road ahead, as if the straight-shot highway took every ounce of his concentration. She was right. He could see the facts how he wanted, just as the judge could. So did that mean he wanted the babies to be his? He couldn't answer that. He didn't know. But with each hour he and Josie and Troy spent together, the more he could imagine being the little guy's dad. The more he could imagine something between him and Josie. And the more he felt those might not be bad things.

"How about Jimmy?"

"How about him?"

"He's in love with her, you know."

He hadn't thought about it when he and Honey were dating, but he couldn't deny it now.

"And judging from the way he reacted, he slept with Honey, too. After you told her you were leaving."

He held up a hand. "You don't have to spell it out. I get it. Jimmy could be the babies' father, too. But he wouldn't send some guy with a gun after her."

"You sure he's not the jealous type?"

"I can't imagine it." But then just a few days ago, he couldn't imagine himself as a father, either. Now it was getting, not easy, but possible.

"Jealousy would give him motive whether the babies are his or not. He loves her, and if she didn't return that love…" She let her voice trail off, allowing him to fill in the rest.

A weight descended on his shoulders. Jimmy was jealous of him. He always had been. But Honey had trusted Jimmy. He was her friend. Her confidant. It had been hard for her to make girlfriends. With women, she'd always felt competitive, and most of them had been jealous of her. It was no wonder she didn't trust them. But she'd trusted Jimmy. The thought that she might now be running from him was tragic.

He glanced in the rearview mirror. The same green pickup trailed behind that he'd seen after they'd driven by Honey's apartment. "Strange."

"What is it?"

"What do you think the odds are of a car following our exact path from Dallas to Springton?"

She twisted in her seat, straining to see out the back window. "Which one?"

"The green truck."

"Are you sure it's following us?"

"Pretty sure. And it looks a lot like the one I thought was following us yesterday." He eased over into the exit lane. "This ought to give us an answer."

Springton was pretty small, as far as bedroom communities around Dallas went. It was made up of a few housing developments and a handful of ranches on the outskirts. Big ranches like Wexler Ranch and tiny like the Double Kay. There wouldn't be too many people with business in this area. The truck shouldn't take the exit.

The truck's yellow turn signal flashed to life. It eased into the exit lane.

Josie drew in a sharp breath. "What do you want to do?"

He knew what he wanted to do. Make an abrupt stop, climb out of the car, tire iron in hand, and beat the crap out of whoever was playing this game. Unfortunately he wasn't sure about the location of the rental's tire iron. "Too bad you couldn't bring your gun."

"You think it's the guy from San Francisco? You think he followed us here?"

"It's possible. It's probably not the judge's people."

"How do you know that?"

"Lawyers don't drive pickup trucks."

"That only works if you believe he only has lawyers out looking for Honey."

The highway morphed into a country road. Soon, instead of tall buildings, parking lots and shopping malls, they were surrounded by pasture and tangles of mesquite.

"He just switched on his turning signal. He's turning into that driveway.

Reed let out a breath he didn't realize he was holding. "Must be a rancher."

He could feel Josie's glance, as if she wasn't sure she believed that, either. At least he wasn't the only one who was paranoid. Paranoia might be the thing that kept them alive.

Josie collapsed back in her seat, but the tension filling the car didn't let up. "Maybe our luck is changing."

"Maybe." Only Reed wasn't sure what it was changing to.

Chapter Ten

Reed had seen some beautiful spreads in his years growing up in Texas, but none outdid the Wexler Ranch. He'd heard about the place first from his mother. She'd even taken him driving past it every month or so, so he could see what a real ranch looked like, she'd said. In his teenage years, the place had been a legend in his high school, mainly a result of the bragging of Teddy Wexler, Jr. The place had seemed like a kingdom to a kid from the Double Kay. White board fence, a rare luxury around these parts. Ten thousand head of cattle. A house built as a carbon copy of the White House, maybe even more grand. Two outdoor swimming pools for summer and one inside for use during the colder months. Tennis courts and—the most amazing thing of all—a full-sized football field right there in the backyard, so Teddy Jr. could practice his state-champion passing form.

Reed couldn't see the football field from the home's circular drive, but the mansion still looked every bit important enough to house the president himself. And he couldn't help feeling a little awed at the white board fence, even as an adult.

He parked the car, and they marched to the front entrance. The doorbell chime was still echoing when the door swung wide. A maid, complete with gray dress and white apron, stood in the opening. Black hair pulled back from her face in a thick braid. "May I help you?"

Her Mexican accent made Reed think of Esme. "Is Mrs. Wexler home?"

"Who should I say is calling?"

"Reed Tanner and J. R. Dionne...from the Double Kay Ranch," he added.

"Thank you." She shut the door, leaving them staring at the leaded glass and white molding.

"So his house is as pretentious as the man himself. Can I expect his wife to be the same?"

"Not sure. She wasn't on the scene yet when Teddy Jr. and I were in high school. She's the judge's second wife. And except for the Springton Stallions' games, my family and the Wexlers didn't exactly run in the same social circles."

"I noticed what I assume was her picture in the judge's chambers. Miss Texas?"

He hadn't remembered that and hadn't noticed the photo, but it didn't surprise him. "It seems you have to earn a spot in the judge's family. No trophies, no inheritance."

Josie let out a sigh. "If he is the twins' father, I can see why Honey wouldn't want him anywhere near them."

Reed set his chin. He still wouldn't believe the judge had fathered Troy. The man would have to come up with proof.

The door swung open once more, and the maid beckoned them into the house his mother would have killed to be able to visit. The air-conditioning hit with the chill of an arctic blast. They followed her across the white marble floor of the foyer and into a parlor decorated with a combination of crown moldings and thick rugs that would look at home on Pennsylvania Avenue and paintings of horses and landscapes that were pure-D Texas.

Portia Wexler sat on a love seat near a blazing fire. She wore a gold dress that showed off her tiny waist and had the fancy look of some sort of designer original. Its skirt flared out over the velvet of the love seat. Between that and the way she tilted her head to the side and twisted her body just so, she looked like a doll on display.

The maid made introductions and stepped back to the edge of the room.

Portia offered them a beauty-queen smile. She was a good-looking woman. Sleek blond hair, sparkling blue eyes and high-as-the-sky cheekbones. But there was something brittle about her Reed couldn't quite put his finger on. She really did look like a doll. Gorgeous, but with the fragility of china. She reminded him of his mother.

"Nice to meet you, Reed, J.R. It's always nice to get a visit from a neighbor. Please, sit down." She gestured to a seating area facing her.

A neighbor? That was generous. The only thing the Double Kay had in common with the Wexler Ranch was a poling place. Reed lowered himself into one of the most uncomfortable chairs he'd ever sat on. Josie perched beside him on a chair with curlicue legs.

"Did Louisa offer you sweet tea? Louisa?"

Reed shook his head. He sure as hell couldn't accept this woman's hospitality, not while knowing the bomb they were going to drop on her. "Thank you, but it's not necessary. We're not going to be here that long."

"Oh, you don't have to rush off so quickly you can't have a little refreshment. Poor things."

"I would love some sweet tea."

Reed turned to Josie.

She shrugged. "I've always wanted to try it."

"Marvelous." Portia Wexler beamed. "Louisa?"

The maid rushed from the room.

"Now, to what do I owe the pleasure of your visit?"

Reed pressed against the stiff back of his chair. How in the hell did you break the news that her husband thought he'd fathered babies with another woman? His mouth felt dry as sand. Maybe he should have taken her up on that sweet tea. "We just have a few questions to ask, if you don't mind."

"Of course I don't mind. However I can help…"

Clearing her throat, Josie leaned forward, hands on knees. "Do you know a woman by the name of Honey Dawson?"

A shadow seemed to pass across Portia's brittle features. She blinked, then smiled all the wider. "The name sounds familiar. Sorry, I can't place it at the moment. Who is she?"

"She's a friend of your husband's."

"My husband has a lot of friends. He's a very influential man."

"Honey would be a special friend. Young. Blond. Pregnant."

Reed shifted his feet in the thick, cream-colored rug. He wanted to stand, to walk, to get out of this stiff room, this frigid house. He knew Josie was trying to break through Portia's defenses, shock her into blurting out a truth she'd rather hide, much as he'd attempted to

do with the judge. But that didn't mean he enjoyed witnessing it.

"Teddy does give money to a charity to help unfor-
tunate girls like that." Portia gave an innocent smile, as
if that must be the answer Josie was looking for, because
it was the only one to be had.

"Did he give her money?"

"You'll have to check with the charity. I don't know
anything about Teddy's donations."

"This didn't come through any charity, Mrs. Wexler."

"I don't know what you mean."

"Let me explain it to you, then."

The sound of ice cubes pinging against crystal rang
through the room like pealing bells. Louisa scurried
across the thick rug with the tray of sweet tea.

Reed let out a long breath. He wasn't built for this kind
of warfare, at least not between women. Words that cut.
Inflections of voice. Subtle shades of a smile. Give him
a muddy field and eleven men dying to kill him for their
chance at the pigskin in his hands. That he understood.

As Louisa served Josie her tea, Reed looked for a
gentler way to get the answers they needed. "Honey
Dawson is missing, and your husband has hired some
lawyers to find her."

He tried to ignore the pointed look Josie shot his way.

Portia covered her mouth with manicured fingers.
"Missing? The poor girl. There's no reason to worry, is
there?"

"No. I'm sure she's fine." He wasn't sure of anything
after their run-in with the man in San Francisco, least
of all that. But there seemed no point in explaining his
concerns to Portia.

"I don't understand. If you're wondering what Teddy has found, why don't you ask him? He won't be home for hours now, but you can probably find him at the courthouse."

Josie set her untasted tea on the tray in front of her. "We've already seen your husband. We came to talk to you."

"And how can I possibly help you?"

Reed braced himself.

Josie lifted her chin. "Honey Dawson gave birth to twins, a boy and a girl. Your husband seems to think he's the father." She paused, as if to let the words sink in.

Portia's smile never faltered.

"We're sorry to have to spring it on you like this, Mrs. Wexler." Reed meant it. She hadn't shown a stitch of emotion, but he knew the lack of outward signs didn't mean Portia Wexler wasn't hurting from the news. His mother had been like that. And he had a sense Portia was very much like her in that way, too. Hell, the poor woman was probably in shock.

Josie stared a hole through the woman, seemingly not sorry at all. "Your husband said he hired people to find Honey and her babies. We need to know why."

Portia tilted her head, as if looking at Josie from a different angle would help her understand. "Why? Why what?"

"Why did he hire them? To find his children? Or to make sure they were never found again?"

Portia splayed a hand on her chest. For the first time she looked as if she suspected their visit might be more than a friendly social call. "Pardon me? I don't know what kind of bone you have to pick with my husband, dear, but how can you possibly suggest he would do such a dastardly thing?"

Reed could answer that one. He could never understand going to the extreme of hurting someone in order to keep a secret, but he could understand the urge that might be behind it. "How about to protect you? Might he want to make the problem go away in order to keep you from finding out? Keep you from getting hurt?"

Portia reached across the corner of the glass table and patted him on the knee. "That's sweet. Bless your heart."

Even if the judge didn't care about protecting Portia, Reed was pretty sure he was still interested in protecting himself. "Could that be the case?" He tried to ignore Josie's glare boring through him.

"I'm afraid not."

Of all the things he'd expected her to say, that wasn't one. "What? Why not?"

"I do recall the name Honey Dawson. Yes, I believe I do." She plucked a glass from the tray and took a long sip of tea.

"And your husband's efforts to find her and her babies? Are those details coming back to you, too?"

Portia smiled at Josie's sarcastic tone. Apparently the woman was not going to back down or drop her friendly façade, no matter how much Josie pushed. "Why, yes. I believe they are."

"Well?"

She glanced around the room. "This is a big house. An empty house, really. It needs some spark, some life. What better way than to fill these walls with children's laughter?"

Josie sputtered. "You're saying you'd welcome

another woman's children into your home? Children she had by your husband?"

Portia gave her a benevolent smile. "Who better for children to be with than their daddy? And who better to raise them than me?"

JOSIE WAS SO ANGRY, she could barely wait until the car doors were closed. "What the hell was that?"

"What was what?" He had the nerve to look at her with those big hazel eyes, now an innocent shade of green.

Fake innocence. As fake as Portia's waxing on about the joys of family the twins would bring to her life. "Why did you make things easy on her?"

"Easy? Hearing your husband might have fathered twins with another woman? You call that easy?"

"She wasn't surprised. Not for a second."

"Even so, it couldn't be fun."

"I don't care if Portia Wexler was having fun or not. I wanted answers. I wanted the truth. I thought you wanted that, too."

"Of course I do."

"Then why did you try to namby-pamby the guts out of everything I asked her?"

Reed looked down at the wheel as if he was going to turn the key in the ignition, yet he didn't move. He shook his head. "I need to get out of Texas."

"What? Why?"

One second passed, then another, stretching like minutes.

"Does this have something to do with the past?" She was taking a shot in the dark, but she wanted to know. She sensed something in him, something that only grew stronger since they'd come to Dallas. To the ranch. He seemed distressed. In pain. Not the cocky sailor she'd known in San Francisco, but someone very different. Someone he was trying to cover up.

He started the car. "In the end, we got our answers anyway."

So that was that. The moment was gone, and she had less of a clue as to what made him tick than ever.

She shook her head and settled back into her seat as he piloted the car down the long, white-fenced drive. "Don't tell me you believe her."

"Do I believe she wants to be a mother? That she's eager to fill her empty house with the children her husband had with other women?" He glanced at her from the corner of his eye and shot her a grin worthy of that sailor. "Not a chance."

She folded her arms across her chest. "Well, thank God. Now I don't have to kick your ass."

A chuckle sounded from deep in his chest. "I don't know, that might be fun."

She could feel the heat start to creep up her neck. What was with her? A suggestive comment, and she turned into a blushing little twit. Hoping he didn't notice, she looked out the window. Something green caught her eye in the rearview mirror. "That truck."

Reed looked in the rearview to see what she was referring to and cursed under his breath.

She wished she had her gun. But without a Texas private-investigator's license, she couldn't function here as anything other than a private citizen. A private citizen without a concealed-carry permit.

Reed slowed the car.

"What are you doing?"

"I'm going to find out who's driving that damn truck. And what he wants."

"How?"

He swung the car around a bend in the road obscured by stunted, twisted trees and stopped. Unfastening his safety belt with one hand, he unlatched the trunk and reached for the door handle with the other.

"You can't go out there." Josie grabbed his arm.

He threw open the door. "Don't worry."

"But he could have a—"

"Scrunch down in the seat." He got out, circled to the trunk and opened it. Pulling something free, he strode into the tangle of brush.

He was crazy. Insane.

The pop of tires on gravel sounded from behind.

Blood pulsing in her ears, Josie slid low in her seat and peered out the passenger-side window. In the mirror, she could see a green truck stopped behind their car and the silhouette of a man hulked in the driver's seat.

Objects might be closer than they appear.

She stared at the broad shoulders in the truck. A flash of movement came from the tangle of brush and trees.

Reed.

Chapter Eleven

Reed brought the tire iron down full force on the green truck's hood. Steel crunched under the blow. The impact shuddered up his arm. He circled the truck's hood and caught the edge of the driver's door before the guy could yank it shut. "Why the hell are you following us?"

He looked at Reed with saucer eyes as pale as his redhead complexion. A gurgling sound came from deep in his throat.

Reed hadn't seen Neil Kinney in over a year, but jail hadn't changed the sniveling little bastard one bit. Even though he had fifty pounds on Reed, he cringed back against the seat, his stare glued to the tire iron Reed had grabbed from the rental's trunk. He was a spineless and cowardly creep who chose to harass women because he wasn't strong enough to look a man in the eye.

Reed lifted his makeshift weapon to an even more threatening angle. "Answer, Kinney."

"I...I...I'm looking for her."

"Who?"

"For Honey. For Honey."

"Where is she?"

"I don't know. She's gone. I go to her apartment, and she's never there. Not anymore."

"Why are you following us?"

Josie stepped up beside Reed.

Kinney's gaze flicked to her.

Reed wanted to tell her to get back in the car. He didn't want this guy near her. He didn't know what Kinney knew or didn't know about Honey's disappearance, but the guy gave him the creeps. He didn't want him even looking in Josie's direction. "I asked you a question, Kinney. Keep your eyes on me. Why are you following us?"

"You were gone, now you came back. You went by her place. I thought you might know where she is."

"I'm sure your parole officer would be interested to know you've been following Honey again. Keeping tabs on whoever stops at her apartment."

"Don't tell. Please. I never talk to her or go inside. I just watch out for her. I take care of her."

"Okay, Neil. You want to watch out for Honey?"

"Yes." Kinney put his hands on the steering wheel. His fingers trembled.

"Then tell me who else has been at her apartment. Who have you seen?"

"Her friend. The one who works in the court."

"Jimmy Bartow," Josie supplied.

"The judge. He has other people there sometimes. Lawyers."

"Who else?"

"Women."

Cheerleaders, perhaps. Even though Honey didn't have many female friends, he knew she wouldn't give up on her dreams to be a cheerleader someday. She'd keep what connections she had alive. Learn the new steps. Plot ways she could make it through auditions and training camp next year. "Good-looking women?"

"I don't know what you mean."

"Get off it, Kinney. Were they nice looking, like cheerleaders, like Honey?"

"Yes. But none look as good as Honey."

"What color hair did they have?"

"Brunette, blond. They were yelling."

Yelling. Interesting. Tiffany Maylor was a brunette. And Reed could see her getting in a yelling match with Honey. He'd witnessed it before. The woman had about as much subtlety as a brickbat.

Or a tire iron.

He lowered the weapon and stepped back from the truck. He would make good on his promise to call Kinney's parole agent, get the creep off the streets, if he could. In the meantime he had a cheerleader to track down. A cheerleader more than capable of hiring the man they'd met in San Francisco. "Get out of here, Kinney. And if you follow us again, I'll use this thing on your head."

JOSIE WAS STILL A LITTLE out of breath by the time they reached Dallas. Reed's stunt with the tire iron had both impressed and unnerved her. And she wasn't sure what to think of how Captain Gorgeous seemed to be morphing into a larger-than-life cowboy type in front of her eyes.

She'd been so wrong when she'd believed he was a simple, commitment-phobic bachelor. He had a lot to him, layer after layer that she didn't have the first clue about. But under it all there seemed to be a hurt, a sadness, he was determined to cover with bravado. And it disturbed her that she wanted so badly to know what it was.

She liked to be in control. She liked to determine what happened next in her life. But ever since she met Troy, she'd been losing control of her heart a little each day. And whenever she was around Reed, she felt as if she was in some kind of crazy free fall. And as exciting as that was, as invigorating, she just had to make sure she didn't crash and burn.

She clamped down on her thoughts and focused on the task ahead. When they'd reached the city they'd tracked down the apartment Tiffany Maylor shared with a redhead, only to find out Tiffany was out partying—a fact that wasn't so surprising. But the fact that she was partying with Teddy Wexler, Jr., was a little more interesting.

By the time they'd reached Teddy Jr.'s condo deep in the heart of the glitziest area of Dallas, the baking Texas sun was disappearing over the horizon. Josie looked up at the building. Almost solid glass, the high-rise condo reflected the late afternoon sun, looking like a solid spire of fire. "Don't you have to be buzzed in to a place like this?"

Reed shrugged. "We'll figure out another way."

They needn't have worried. A young blonde who could rival Honey in looks blocked the elevator door open and gave Reed a big smile that grated along Josie's nerves. "Are you going to the party?"

"Sure are." Reed grabbed Josie's hand and they jumped on board and zoomed to the building's top floor.

Music was throbbing from Teddy Jr.'s condo, and many more glamorous women filled the room. Josie glanced around, feeling short and top-heavy. In this sea of beautiful women, it would be a miracle if they found Tiffany. But Teddy Jr. was much easier to locate.

One hip cocked, he leaned against a chrome-and-black bar in the living room, a highball glass in one hand. He looked just like his father—handsome enough but with a touch of snideness about him that left a greasy feel in the air. His dark hair and height reminded her of Reed, but that's where the similarity ended.

His lips twisted into a smirk. "Tanner, isn't it? Hell of a long time since I've seen you. What are you doing here?"

"Have a few questions for you, Teddy. First off, is Tiffany Maylor around?"

"Tiff? Hell if I know." The younger Teddy Wexler threw his arm around a redhead who'd gotten her magenta locks straight from her hairdresser. His gaze flicked over Josie and landed square on her chest. A little smile curved one side of his mouth, as if with one glance he thought he knew all about her…and one thing he knew without question was that she belonged to him. "Who's the babe?"

What she wouldn't give to smack some reality into this neanderthal. "J. R. Dionne. I'm a private investigator."

"Private. I like that. Wanna investigate me in private?" He didn't bother to raise his eyes to her face.

"So I hear your father had a thing with Honey Dawson?" Reed took a step forward, angling his body toward Josie as if to claim her.

A thrill shimmered up Josie's spine. Suddenly she was having trouble focusing on what Teddy said or did or if Tiffany Maylor was in the room or not. She could think only about how close Reed was. Close enough to put his arm around her shoulder. Close enough to lean in for a kiss.

God help her.

Teddy Jr.'s eyes snapped to Reed. "Honey Dawson? That bimbo? I don't care about brains, if you know what I mean, but nailing her would be like making love to a rock. Guess my old man's standards have slipped. If he had any to begin with."

The magenta-haired beauty giggled and snuggled in tighter to Teddy's side.

"Do you know all this about Honey from experience?" Josie asked.

Teddy's lips twisted in something that resembled a snarl. "I have my standards." As if to prove just how low they were, he gave Miss Magenta an openmouthed kiss.

Interesting. And easy to see through his kissing game. They could cross Teddy Jr. off the list of men who had slept with Honey. Not that the fact made him happy. Nor did it make him less of a suspect in Honey's disappearance, not that they'd considered him before. But just as with Jimmy or Neil Kinney, jealousy could be a powerful motivator.

Teddy brought his steel-gray gaze back to the cleavage she wasn't showing. "So why are you hanging out with this second-string loser when you could be with me?"

Josie could guess the come-ons had more to do with Teddy's rivalry with Reed than it did with her, large chest or not.

"Honey Dawson, Teddy," Reed cut in. "Why is your father trying to find her?"

He shrugged a shoulder. "Hell if I know. She doesn't seem worth it to me."

Judging from the expression on Reed's face, he

wasn't buying the Teddy-doesn't-care-about-Honey bit, either. "So you know nothing about the fact that Honey gave birth to twins? Twins your father says are his?"

"Right," Teddy drawled.

Josie shot him a frown. "You don't believe the babies are his?"

"No."

"Why not?"

"My old man has a lot of money, and Honey Dawson is a gold digger. Pure and simple. He gets a lot of action for an old guy, but he's not stupid."

It was a good point. Josie would think the judge would be careful to use birth control. He was a married man, after all. Still, as eager as he seemed to produce more little trophy winners as a testament to his glory, he could have planned to get Honey pregnant all along. "How much does your mother know about Honey and the twins?"

Teddy Jr. gave her a smirk. "Portia is my stepmother."

"Okay, your stepmother. How much does she know?"

"I don't have a damn clue. There are some things Portia chooses not to know."

"And the fact that your father has affairs is one of them?"

"Oh, darlin', you're not from around here, are you? I don't think anyone could keep her head buried that deep in the sand. Even Portia."

That only left the solution to the problem. Making the babies and Honey disappear. "Does Portia want those babies, too?"

He lifted one shoulder in a shrug. "Portia wants the easy life. Just like I do. I don't see that including kids, do you?"

She couldn't argue with that one. As much as she ached to have a family, it wasn't because she thought it would be easy. In fact, taking care of Troy had given her a taste of how tough, and worth it, it could be.

Teddy flashed a smile at Reed. "Here's a question you can answer for me, Tanner. You were the one screwing Honey. Those babies should belong to you, shouldn't they? Or weren't you up to the job?"

Before Josie knew what was happening, Reed had balled his hand into a fist and smashed it square into Teddy Jr.'s nose.

BOBBY COLLECTED HIS BAG from the carousel and made for the airport's exit to catch a cab. Lights twinkled in the night beyond the glass doors. As he stepped from the airport, the heat of the city hit him broad in the face.

It was nice to be back in Dallas.

San Francisco probably had its good points, but he sure hadn't seen any of them. Cold, windy weather. A damp fog that chilled the humor straight out of him. And far too many men holding other men's hands for this Texas boy's comfort.

No wonder he hadn't been able to get the job done.

He'd had to ditch the weapons he'd bought in California. Tanner and the busty blonde had gotten a pretty good look at him, first at Fisherman's Wharf and then in Chinatown. If they did manage to give the cops a decent description, the last thing he wanted was for them to find any kind of weapons on him.

No matter. The client had bought them anyway, and the client had money to burn. But if he wanted to get

Chapter Twelve

Josie pulled a bag of frozen okra from the freezer. Judging from the solid lump of ice crystals cementing the pieces of vegetable together, the bag had been in the freezer since long before Reed had moved from the ranch. It would have to do. At least she wasn't planning to eat it.

She brought the bag into the living room, where Reed sat on the couch, feeding Troy. He held the bottle tight in his palm, his long fingers wrapping around the entire circumference, gripping it hard, as if life itself depended on not letting it go.

Troy sucked ferociously, arms flailing. In the baby's agitated state, Josie would be willing to bet he was swallowing as much air as formula. "You need to relax. He's picking up on your stress."

"I'm not stressed."

"Right." She pulled the bottle from his hand and flopped the bag of okra on his purple knuckles. "Hold it to your eye. For the swelling."

"Thanks." He brought the bag to his face. Flinching, he settled back in the threadbare couch.

She gathered Troy from his lap and plopped down next to him. "That will teach you not to fight."

"Teddy Jr. is an ass."

"No argument on that from me. That doesn't mean you had to be an ass, too." Their visit to Teddy Jr.'s condo had degenerated into a fistfight between the two men, stopped only by a couple of strapping football types pulling them apart. They hadn't been able to ask any more questions, and they never did find Tiffany Maylor.

"Oh, come on. You liked seeing me be an ass. It's better than just standing there and letting him spew his crap."

Some part of her knew she should be horrified by the stupid show of swaggering, testosterone-fueled violence. But the truth was, it had kind of turned her on. But then, everything about Reed seemed to turn her on, a tendency that was really starting to worry her. "I like to imagine there are other ways to handle people like Teddy Jr. Better ways."

"You like to imagine? And here I didn't think you had an imagination."

At his teasing, a flutter moved through her stomach despite her best efforts to squelch it. The problem was, she had plenty of imagination. Way too much. Just looking at him leaning back in the couch, his T-shirt hugging his tight stomach and stretching over his shoulders, made her imagine running her fingers under the cotton. The way his legs splayed wide made imagining anything but what was under the bulge in those jeans impossible. And that mischievous smirk on his face...

She shook her head and looked down at the baby. If she needed a reminder of how serious this case was, how mismatched she and Reed were, she had only to look into Troy's tender face. They wanted different things. She wanted a family, and she didn't have a clue what he wanted. Maybe he didn't, either.

No, the only thing they did have in common was this case. They needed to find Honey. They needed to discover who was behind the threat to her and her twins and the attack on Missy. And she needed to keep this crazy crush she had on Reed Tanner under wraps. "So what is the whole story between you and Teddy Wexler, Jr.?"

The grin fell from his lips. "You saw the picture. We went to the same high school, both played football."

"Now, I can't imagine that." Reed was tall and fit, but he wasn't exactly the body type she associated with football. "You're not bulky enough."

"In these parts, everyone plays football. Or at least every boy who's good enough to make the team."

"And you both were?"

"We both went out for quarterback. But his daddy is important. Mine ran out on my mother before I was born."

"So you were rivals. There's a lot of that rivalry thing going on around here, isn't there?"

He looked at her as if he had no idea what she was referring to.

"You and Teddy Jr. Honey and that other cheerleader."

"Tiffany Maylor."

"It must be something in the water."

He gave a short laugh that sounded a little hollow.

She couldn't figure him out. With all the secrets people around here seemed to be keeping, she couldn't help feeling Reed was hiding the most. "Was that important to you? Being first-string?"

He gave her a puzzled look. "That was high school. I've gotten over it."

"Sure you have. That's why you just started a brawl in the middle of a party. Were you rivals for Honey, too?"

"Anything Teddy Jr. had with Honey was in his imagination. He asked her out while she was with me, and she turned him down. End of story."

"But she got involved with his father."

Reed lifted the bag of okra from his face with his good hand and flexed his bruised fingers, grimacing.

"Why do you think she did that?"

"If I had to guess? I'd say it was money and influence. Maybe even more influence than money."

"What do you mean?"

"The judge is a powerful guy. He can make things happen around here."

"Like he did for his son."

"Right. I'm betting after Honey was cut from the cheerleading squad, she wanted to even the odds for next year."

"Even the odds?"

"Tiffany Maylor has a wealthy and powerful father. Owns a string of jewelers. Runs in the same circles as Jerry Jones himself. Honey probably figured it wouldn't hurt to have some political clout on her side. Balance the odds."

"Did she mention that to you?"

"Did she say she planned to have sex with the judge? Of course not. Did she wish out loud she could even the odds? All the time."

Josie considered all he'd told her and all she'd seen at the courthouse and the Wexler Ranch. It didn't add up. She could understand the rivalry between him and

Teddy Jr., a rivalry that Jimmy Bartow seemed to feel toward Reed as well, though for a different reason. But what about Reed's reaction to Portia Wexler? How did that fit into any of this? There was more. A lot more he was holding back. "So how about you and Portia?"

"Me and Portia? I don't know Portia. Never met her before today."

"Why did he and his first wife divorce?"

"If you believe rumors, Portia filled Honey's role back then."

"She had an affair with the judge?"

"Until he got his divorce and married her."

"Do you think she would hire someone to go after Honey and the babies?"

"Maybe. That means the guy in San Francisco was lying when he told Missy he was working for the babies' father."

"You know, there's still the chance that you're the babies' father."

He nodded. No tightening of his expression. No looking away. "And I didn't hire anyone. So sure, Portia could be on the list. So could Tiffany Maylor." He laid his hand on a thigh and balanced the okra on top.

He had a point. But Josie didn't want to talk about the cheerleader. She needed to know what was behind his reaction to Portia. And she needed to know for personal reasons she didn't care to examine too closely. "You still haven't explained what happened at the ranch. Why did you try to defend Portia from my questions?"

"I wasn't trying to defend her."

Now, that was an evasion even he had to recognize. She lowered her chin and stared up at him.

"Okay, okay. Why do you think I was trying to defend her?"

Truth was, she didn't know. On the way back to Reed's ranch, she'd thought his reaction to Portia was caused by some past connection between them. But if he had never even met her until today, that left her with nothing but the crudest of guesses. "You like Portia? You're attracted to her?"

His eyes widened and his mouth opened as if horrified at the idea. "You've got to be kidding me."

"She's an attractive woman. A former beauty queen. And a lot of men like older women."

He held up his injured hand as if to block the idea from reaching him. The bag of frozen okra fell to the hardwood floor. "I do not have the hots for Portia Wexler. If anything, she reminds me of my mother. Now you, on the other hand, are much more to my taste."

The inflection he put on the last word made a shiver of warmth ripple over Josie's skin. But while she couldn't control her traitorous body's response, she was not going to let him get her off track. "So you protecting Portia, does it have something to do with your mother?"

Reed's expression went blank.

Josie could swear the pressure in the air changed. It grew thicker, heavier. She could feel the weight in her chest. "You used to have to take care of your mother, protect her, keep her from getting upset."

"I'm not going to talk about my mother."

"With me?"

"With anyone."

Josie had struck a nerve. She knew that. But she also knew she had only scratched the surface. And she was not going to back off. She looked down at Troy, now sleeping, his head tilted to the side and drool dribbling out one corner of his mouth.

There was too much at stake to agree to Reed's terms.

"I'll just have to ask Esme."

He thrust himself up from the chair. Okra crunching underfoot, he paced across the floor and stopped at the bay window. He stared out the window toward the shabby barn and the metal-pipe fencing, with its peeling paint, that formed the corral. "This case is not about my mother. I don't want you asking Esme or anyone else about her. Got that?"

If there was anything that set Josie off, it was an implied threat. And although she knew she should keep her mouth shut, she couldn't quite manage it. "Or what? What are you going to do if I talk to Esme? If I learn whatever it is you're hiding?"

"I'll hire another investigator."

"Then you'd better start thumbing through the Yellow Pages." She pushed herself out of the couch and carried Troy into the makeshift nursery. She was shaking so badly, she feared she'd wake him. Luckily, he was deep in baby sleep. A bomb probably couldn't rouse him. She lowered him into his crib and strode back to the living room.

Reed hadn't moved from the bay window, but his body language had changed drastically. Instead of rigid, defensive and loaded for bear, his posture seemed apologetic, shoulders tilted forward, head slightly bowed. "My mother was sick for a long time, all right? I was the only one she had."

There she went, sticking foot in mouth once again.

Pressing a point that wasn't her business. She was such a jerk. "A long time? How long was she sick?"

He gave a tense shrug.

"As long as you can remember?"

He didn't answer, didn't turn. He just stared out the window as if he couldn't pull his eyes away.

"What was wrong with her?"

"I told you I don't want to talk about it. It's not important anyway."

"It seems pretty important."

He shook his head. "Not to this case."

She couldn't tell him she was interested in more than this case. She didn't want to admit how interested, even to herself. Reed's flirting comments might be mere fun and games, smoke screens to prevent her from getting too close, or at the most, just a bid to get in her pants for a little fun. But her interest had moved beyond fun, beyond simple sexual attraction. She was really starting to care about him. Feelings she needed to rein in. "Okay then, let's bring it back to the case. How does Portia Wexler remind you of your mother?"

He glanced at her out of the corner of his eye, as if he was aware of her attempt at an end around. "Portia is a needy woman. She needs the people around her to help her live her life. She strikes me as incredibly brittle."

Josie nodded. That sounded like the Portia she'd met. And presumably that's what Reed's mother had been like, as well. "So she's dependent on the judge."

"More than dependent, don't you think? And I'm sure the judge encourages it. The judge likes to be needed."

The conversation with Jimmy played through her mind. "Is that what Honey is like?"

"What do you mean?"

"Jimmy seemed to think you should have supported her more. Did she need a lot of support?"

"I guess, yeah."

The picture of Reed was far from clear, but she was getting an idea of what had made him shy away from responsibility. "Like your mother."

"We're not—"

"Talking about your mother, I know. I also know the judge seems to have chosen two women who would need him, Portia and Honey. Women who might become desperate if he didn't come through for them. Some men like that. Feeling needed. But I know it can be a horrible burden, as well."

"It wasn't her fault. Not all of it. She was depressed. She started drinking after my father left."

"How old were you when he left?"

"I never knew him."

"Who took care of you?"

"Esme. She took care of my mother, too. Until I was old enough to take over."

"I'm sorry. You mother shouldn't have heaped all that on you."

"She couldn't help it. She needed help, only…" His gaze drifted back to the window.

"Only what?" Josie prompted.

"I could never help her enough."

Josie couldn't find the words. It seemed anything she could say would sound trivial compared to what he'd just admitted. No wonder he'd shied away from others' expectations. He'd failed to be enough for his mother. Why would he want to put himself out there only to fail now? "Is that why you moved to San Francisco? To get away?"

"My mother died. That's when I moved."

"I'm sorry." It was starting to seem as if those were the only words she could say.

He shook his head. "The last years were hard. She was sick. In pain. When she finally died, well, I could only feel relieved." He flinched after saying the words.

"That's understandable."

"Is it? I wished for her death." He shook his head again. "That's not understandable. That's wrong."

"Years of failure followed by guilt. What a horrible way to live. I think you did the right thing by moving away."

He turned his head back to face her, but didn't meet her eye. "Maybe the right thing for me. But in the end I abandoned Honey. Just like she'd been abandoned all her life. I even knew it at the time. And I did it anyway."

"It was probably the only thing you could do."

He gave a soft grunt, as if he wasn't about to forgive himself so easily.

"You can't live someone else's life for them. No one can."

"That's nice of you to say. But…"

"But what?"

"But if she was pregnant with my babies, I didn't just abandon Honey. I did exactly what I cursed my father for all these years." He reached out and touched the ends of her hair with his fingertips. "When you said it was time for me to be a man, that's what I thought of. That's why I'm here. I'm not going to be like him."

She didn't know what to say. There wasn't anything she could say. Not anything that would make things better. But she could comfort him. She could make him feel less alone.

She stepped close to him and laid a hand on his arm. Reaching up, she wrapped her arms around his shoulders and pulled him close.

His lips brushed against her cheek as they hugged, and she buried her face in the soft spot between his shoulder and neck. She breathed in his scent, leather with a hint of musk, so stirring, so male. She moved her lips against his neck in a whisper of a kiss.

He turned his head at her touch. His lips found hers, closed over them, claimed them. His tongue pressed between the seam and thrust into her mouth.

Heat washed over her. Longing. Desire so strong it made her knees falter. She shouldn't be doing this. It wasn't smart. It wasn't good for her. But despite the alarm jangling in the back of her mind, she joined her tongue with his and teased him farther into her mouth. Claiming him just as he'd claimed her. Urging his tongue deep.

She'd hugged him in order to comfort him, but that wasn't all she wanted. She wanted him. She wanted him to forget Honey, forget everybody. She wanted him to focus only on her. Her mouth, her breasts, that tender spot between her legs. He made her want to throw away caution and responsibility and the act of reason itself and just feel.

She must be out of her mind.

She closed her eyes and urged the kiss deeper, the strokes of her tongue more insistent, more intimate. She should back away. She should get a grip on her feelings, control her desire, but it seemed impossible. She didn't even know where to start.

His hands moved over her shoulders, down her back. He cupped her buttocks and pulled her tight. His urgency strained against her.

She twined her leg around the outside of his, opening to him, fitting the most sensitive part of her against his hard urgency. She couldn't get close enough. Couldn't feel him deep enough. She wanted him naked against her. Inside her. She needed to feel him thrust deep before thought and reason returned.

She slipped her hands under his shirt and skimmed her fingers over the light sprinkling of hair and the warm skin underneath. Moving down his sides, her fingertips rested on the waistband of his jeans. She grasped his belt buckle, desperate to pull it free, to remove the layers between them.

"Mmm. I like how you think." His voice vibrated low in his chest. Still kissing her, he kneaded her buttocks with one hand. The other worked between their bodies. He unfastened her jeans as if it was no effort at all.

She shook her head. "No. You don't understand."

He pushed her jeans over her hips and down to her knees. "What's to understand?" Another pass of his hands and her panties were out of the way as well. Cool air tickled her most intimate place. Reed's warm hands moved up the back of her thighs and gripped her buttocks once more.

Her thighs moved apart, as if by their own will. She tilted her hips up, pressing against him. The roughness of his jeans made her gasp deep in her throat. "I'm going regret this. I know I am."

"You won't regret it. You might be a little sore by the

time I get done with you, but you won't have any regrets. I promise." His hands moved again, unbuckling his belt, lowering his zipper, pushing his own jeans and briefs down his legs. When he pressed against her again, his erection was warm and smooth and naked.

What had she gotten herself into? This was supposed to be an innocent hug. A show of friendship. Support. "I'm not the type of person who falls into bed with a man I barely know."

"Who said anything about a bed?"

Oh, she couldn't do this. She started to pull back.

Reed held her fast, his erection pressing against her. "Oh, come on. Let loose, Josie. You want me. I know you do. And I sure as hell want you. Throw caution to the wind." He stroked his hardness against her without slipping inside.

Heat spread over her skin and pooled between her legs. Not just heat. An electric charge as well. Energy she'd never felt before. "I don't throw caution to the wind. Not without some kind of plan."

"Maybe it's time you started." With each stroke, his length grew slicker, lubricated by her body. The pleasure built until it bordered on intolerable.

Any moment he was going to be inside her. Any moment she would lose all control. Of her body. Of her thoughts. Of her heart. Control she would never be able to regain. "Wait."

The delicious movement slowed.

"Please, Reed."

He stopped and pulled back from their kiss. Brows knitting, he searched her eyes. "Are you okay?"

"I can't…" Her protest died in her throat. She couldn't.

She knew that. Yet she wanted this more than anything she'd wanted in a long time.

"You're right," he said, his voice gentle and understanding yet with a note of teasing. Flirting. "It can't happen this way."

She blew a breath through tense lips. She knew what she wanted. For him to take responsibility. To end this crazy thing between them so she didn't have to. Because right now, she doubted she had the strength.

"No, if we're going to do this, I want to see you."

That wasn't what she was hoping for, but a thrill of excitement rippled through her body nonetheless.

His fingers moved under her T-shirt and whispered along her skin.

Every nerve fired to life. Her heart thrummed in her chest. She should stop him. She had to stop him. But all she could focus on was the slick heat between her legs and the rasp of rough fingers on her skin.

He slid her shirt up, over her shoulders, over her head. Dropping it on the floor, he moved his hands over the cups of her bra. His fingers teased her nipples; the texture of the silky fabric between them only heightened the sensation.

He moved against her again. Stroking her with his length. Coming so close to penetrating her, to possessing her, she moaned with want she couldn't let herself feel. His movement grew faster, more insistent.

Heat shuddered through her body with the power of an electric shock. A hum filled her mind. Another ripple seized her muscles. Her legs wobbled. She gripped his shoulders and held on. She couldn't control her body.

She couldn't control anything at all.

Chapter Thirteen

Reed was ready to bury himself in Josie, lose himself in her heat, feel her shudders from the inside, when she placed her hands firmly against his shoulders and pushed him away. "Josie?" She couldn't pull the plug now. He was so close. He had gotten a good feel of her slippery heat and if he didn't get inside, he was a goner. He wouldn't be able to calm down, no matter how long he stood under a cold shower.

She leaned in and gave him another one of those kisses he could feel all the way to his groin. Then, sliding her hands down his sides, she knelt in front of him and took him into her mouth.

A groan worked its way up from deep inside him.

She moved up and down his length, sucking him deep with one stroke, then skimming over him with just the tip of her tongue on the next. She peered up his body, meeting his eyes as if drawing something intimate out of him with each pull.

If he thought he was going to explode before, it was nothing compared to now. He cupped a hand around the back of her head, stilling her movement.

There was more he wanted. More he wished to explore. "Wait."

She gave him a questioning gaze.

"Your bra. I want to see you."

She released him, leaving him pulsing and glistening and desperate for more. Pushing out her chest, she reached behind her back and unclasped her bra. She slid the straps down her arms, and her breasts spilled free.

For a moment he could do nothing but look. Her chest was big and firm, but not in a plastic way. No, her breasts were real. Soft and lush. Her nipples jutted toward him, erect and hard as if begging him to touch. To taste. The length of him flexed in anticipation.

Josie watched him. Her tongue smoothed over her lips. She moved close again. Her tongue flicked up the sensitive underside of his hardness. Her lips closed around him.

He threaded his fingers through her hair. "Stop, Josie. I can't hold out."

"Who said I wanted you to hold out?" She moved up and down his shaft.

The pressure in his groin built and built. He wanted more. Wanted it to last. Wanted to kiss her, taste her, plunge inside as deep as he could get. He needed to stop her before it was too late, yet that was the last thing he wanted to do.

She took him in her hand and rubbed him over her breasts, over the hard nipples, until he could take no more. She was in control now, dictating to him what she wanted, deciding what each move should be, bringing about the result she chose. He wasn't used to a woman being so outward about taking control. Not at all. He didn't have to guess what she wanted. Didn't have to try to be everything for her. And that made it all the more exciting. And all the more impossible to resist.

With one last gasp, he gave in. But when the pulsing faded and the roar in his ears subsided, he knew this wasn't the end. It was only the beginning. And next time, Josie Renata Dionne would be squirming under his mouth and crying out under his touch. She would feel everything she made him feel tonight, and that was one area in which he knew he wouldn't fail.

JOSIE HAD BEEN RIGHT.

She threw back the covers of a bed she'd tossed and turned in for too few hours, levered herself to her feet, and padded to the bathroom, morning sun streaming over her shoulder. From the moment she'd escaped alone to the guest room, despite Reed's protests, she'd regretted making love with him.

Making love? Not hardly. What they'd done was flat-out, hootchie-cootchie sex. The worst part was, she wanted more. And if that wasn't proof she was cruising for a heartache, she didn't know what was.

What had gotten into her?

She knew the answer. Reed. He affected her that way. Made her want to quit planning and just do. Give up control and just feel.

She twisted on the shower and pulled the T-shirt over her head. She'd never felt so desired, so powerful, so in control—even though she knew she hadn't been in control at all. Hell, just being naked reminded her of Reed, made her want to walk down the hall to his room and experience everything they hadn't done last night.

What would it be like to give herself to him totally? Surrender to her feelings?

She'd have to be crazy.

Sure, there was more to him than she'd first believed. He wasn't some irresponsible playboy. He had a good heart. She'd seen it. But that only made her want him more. It didn't dissolve the barriers between them. He wasn't ready to give her what she wanted—a family. A baby of her own. And she couldn't let herself settle.

But after last night, she couldn't help but wonder if she could be happy without him.

"HE LOOKS LIKE A COP."

Reed leaned down next to Josie and peered out the cracked front bay window. A man slammed the driver's door and circled a car with rental plates. He wasn't wearing a uniform. In fact, to Reed he looked like any other guy. Jeans. A white shirt. But if Josie thought he looked like a cop, who was he to argue? "How do you know?"

"The way he carries himself. His gait says authority."

He stopped and opened the passenger door, waiting for a woman to climb from the car.

"And see how he stands? His shoulders are square, yet his right leg is slightly back. He's protecting his gun side. It's subconscious. He probably isn't even aware he's doing it."

"Why in the hell is a cop here?"

"That I can't tell you."

From a blanket spread out in the center of the living room, Troy sent up a loud squawk.

Reed glanced his way. Judging from the increasing urgency and volume of his complaints, he was getting hungry again. And that meant he would only get louder.

He turned back to the window. He was raised to trust the law, but having grown up here in Springton, he knew that wasn't always the smart course. Especially when you were coming off a fistfight with the son of Judge Teddy Wexler.

"What is it?" Josie asked.

"Can you take Troy into the kitchen? Keep him quiet?"

"You're worried that they've come for the baby?"

"I don't know. But we can't take the chance. The judge has more than a few lawmen in these parts who are willing to do his bidding. No matter what that bidding might be."

Josie's eyes widened with understanding. With a nod, she picked up the baby and scurried for the kitchen.

His squawk echoed down the hall. The little guy ratcheting up his demands. Josie was good with babies, but Reed doubted even she would be able to keep those little vocal chords silent while she warmed his formula.

He headed for the door. He'd have to keep his law-officer visitors out of the house and pray the baby would respond to Josie's appeasement. It might be their only hope for keeping the child's presence from getting back to the judge.

By the time he stepped out onto the porch, the cop had nearly reached the door. A woman with dark, thick hair walked beside him, taking in everything around her in quick glances.

"Reed Tanner?" the man asked.

"Yes."

"John Wise. Samantha Corely. We need to ask you a few questions."

"You're cops?"

"I am." Wise flashed a badge. Not local. Something out of state, although Reed didn't recognize the department. But that explained why the guy drove a rental car. "Ms. Corely works as a children's advocate," Wise added.

Reed's throat tightened. A children's advocate? These people were definitely here about the baby.

"As I understand it, you don't live in this area any longer."

"Right. I moved about a year ago. To San Francisco."

The guy's lips pressed together, and he nodded slightly, as if Reed had given the answer he expected. "And what brings you back?"

The guy was good at hiding his thoughts, but Reed could still tell the question wasn't an innocent one. He was fishing for information. Specifically, information that would incriminate Reed for something at which he could only guess. "I'm tying up some loose ends."

"Loose ends? Explain."

Crap. Probably not the best choice of words. He peered around out over the flat expanse of pasture and tried to organize his thoughts. The real-estate sign swung slightly in the breeze. "I'm putting my mother's ranch on the market."

"You said you moved a year ago. It's taken that long to decide to do this?"

He could clear this up in a second by telling Wise about Esme, but that would only lead to the cop wanting to talk to her. And as painfully honest as Esme was, she would never lie to a police officer. Even if Reed wanted her to. She would tell Wise about the baby. The truth wouldn't work, but maybe he could get the guy to back off another way. "My mother's death was very traumatic. I've needed time to get used to the idea."

"I'm sorry for your loss." The woman's voice was low, her words heartfelt.

Reed nodded his sincere thanks.

The cop wasn't so sympathetic. "I hear you and Honey Dawson had a relationship before you left Texas."

"We did."

"Were you aware that she gave birth to twins a few months ago?"

He knew where Wise was going with this, and he might as well head him off at the pass. "And you're wondering if they're mine?"

The cop arched his brows. "Are they?"

"I don't know."

"But you know about the babies." It wasn't a question. "Honey contacted you about them?"

He paused. He wasn't sure what to answer. Answering yes would only lead to more questions. Answering no would foster suspicion about how he'd learned about the twins. "I got a note from Honey."

The woman piped up. "You haven't seen her? Talked to her?"

"No." It was an honest answer, but he could tell by the way they glanced at one another that they didn't buy it.

"What did the note say?" Wise asked.

"That she had twins. I don't remember the rest."

"I'll bet."

"We have located one of the children," the woman said.

The girl? They'd found her? "Where is she? Where did you find her?"

Wise's brows arched. "How did you know the baby we've located is a girl?"

They had him. He didn't know how he was going to get out of this one.

"Where is the other baby, Tanner?"

"I don't know."

"You don't know, or you're not telling?" Wise asked. Samantha Corely peered past him as if trying to see in the front window of the house.

Damn. Damn. Damn. He was stuck. If they insisted on going in, looking around, what was he going to tell them? His only defense was a good offense. "How did you know I was in town?"

"We talked to a friend of yours."

He narrowed his eyes. "A friend? What friend?"

"Theodore Wexler, Jr. It seems the two of you had a reunion at his condo last night."

"A reunion? That's what he called it?"

"You did a number on his nose. And I can see he got a few licks in, too."

Reed resisted the urge to bring his hand to the bruise under his eye. "If you want to look at someone who could hurt Honey, Teddy Jr. would be a good place to start. Not here."

"Interesting. He said you might tell us that."

"Gee, if a Wexler said it, then you know it has to be true. What else did he say?"

"He said the two of you talked about Honey and her babies last night at the party. He said that you went into a jealous rage."

Reed wished Josie was out here with him. She could give them a very different perspective on Teddy Jr., a perspective they'd be far more likely to listen to than anything he had to say. "I have no reason to be jealous."

"Really? That's not what he said. He told us you've had it in for him ever since he beat you out for quarterback in high school."

He couldn't deny it. Not that they'd believe him, whether he was telling the truth or not.

"He said your animosity extends to his father, as well."

The judge. Of course they had to bring him up. No doubt he was the reason they were here, although Reed never realized his reach extended outside the state of Texas.

"And his stepmother told us you visited her. She's confirmed everything he said."

So much for his trying to make things easier on Portia. Josie would have a good I-told-you-so laugh over that. "So why are you here? To arrest me?" He knew he'd been taking a chance yesterday, asking the Wexlers uncomfortable questions. He'd underestimated how quickly they would act to shut him up. But that didn't mean he would change anything he'd done.

"We'd like to take a look inside the house."

"Get a warrant."

John Wise didn't look surprised at his response. "You're making yourself look guilty of everything Teddy Wexler, Jr. accused."

"You've given me no way around that."

"Just tell us the truth," Samantha Corely said in that low, soothing voice. "Help us find Honey. Help us find her baby. Please."

He wanted to trust her, even though he knew that was the last thing he dared do. "I'm looking for Honey, too. That's the real reason I'm here. I'm worried something has happened to her."

"Why? What prompted your worry?"

He couldn't tell them about the baby. But maybe he could tell them the rest. He had little other choice. "A few days ago, Honey came to my boat in San Francisco, but she left before I arrived. I haven't been able to find any sign of her since."

"So you saw her a few days ago?" The cop's voice was hard, not a bit understanding or soothing.

Reed forced himself to look the man square in the eye. "No. I never saw her. I haven't seen her since I left the Dallas area a year ago. I'm looking for her, too."

"So you were in San Francisco?"

"Yes. I flew here two days ago."

"And you went nowhere else in between?"

"No. I took a flight straight here."

"Can anyone confirm that?"

He dug out his wallet, found his baggage-claim ticket and handed it to the cop. "I filed a report with the San Francisco police the day before I left, and I hired a private investigator to help look for Honey. She was with me on the flight."

"What's her name? Can we talk to her?"

"J. R. Dionne. But she's not here at the moment. I can have her call you, if you give me a number."

John Wise narrowed his eyes, as if he sensed Reed wasn't being totally straight. He thrust the baggage-claim ticket back into Reed's hands. "If you've been looking for Honey, tell me what you've found?"

"Judge Teddy Wexler thinks the babies are his. He says he wants to raise them. And he has lawyers looking for Honey."

The details didn't seem to surprise either of them in the least. "Is there anyone else you can think of that might want to hurt Honey?"

The creepy feeling again assaulted the back of Reed's neck. "Neil Kinney."

Wise clenched his teeth, as if he'd heard the name before. "What is his involvement with Honey?"

"One-sided. He started by peeping in her windows and following her everywhere she went. He moved on to rifling through her underwear drawer. He did time for burglary for that one."

"Where is he now?"

"Here. He was following us yesterday. He drives a green pickup with a big dent in the hood." Reed wasn't sure if they believed his assessment of Kinney or just thought he was trying to deflect suspicion from himself. But he might as well give them the information he had. If they really were looking for Honey, he wanted to give them all the help he could. "Tell me one thing."

John Wise and Samantha Corely both focused intently on him, though again Wise took the lead. "What?"

"The baby girl. Is she okay? Is she safe?"

"Yes," Samantha said. "And I can assure you, she'll stay that way."

He looked down at the dirty gravel under his feet. He might or might not be the babies' father, but either way, he'd never expected knowing that little girl was okay would mean so much. "Thanks."

DUST CURLED INTO THE air, kicked up by a car approaching on the gravel drive. Bobby Crabb frowned. Not Tanner's rental. The client had told him the cowboy sailor and his chesty blonde were driving a small Ford. No, this was someone new leaving the ranch. A couple, judging by the silhouettes in the car. Tanner had had a visitor.

Bobby put his foot back on the gas pedal of his black pickup and kept moving down the highway. Safer to let the car pass. After they were long gone, he could double back and take care of business. Three were definitely easier to control and eliminate than five.

He pulled to the side of the road and watched the car in his rearview mirror. It stopped at the end of the drive, then swung out onto the highway and moved in the opposite direction. He did a cursory check of the rifle leaning against the seat next to him.

This time he wouldn't let Tanner or the babe get in his way. This time nothing would stop him. This time he was hunting on his own turf, and he was about to bag himself a hefty chunk of change.

Chapter Fourteen

Josie wanted to hug Reed. "So Troy's sister. She's all right."

A relieved smile played at the corners of his mouth, but his brow still furrowed with worry. "At least we know that."

Cracking open one side of the bay window once she'd settled the baby with his bottle, she had listened in on his conversation with John Wise and Samantha Corely. She knew she was taking a chance. Troy was happily devouring his bottle, but had he let out a random squeal or laugh, their presence might have been given away. She'd been lucky. Not only had he been a hungry little angel, but she'd been able to hear the good news. And witness Reed's reaction.

He'd said he wasn't the family type, that he didn't know what to do with babies, that he wouldn't be a good father. But the way he'd asked after the baby girl…his reaction to the news that she was safe… The concern and deep relief she'd heard in his voice weren't the reactions of a man who didn't have the capacity or desire to be a daddy.

She closed her eyes and pulled in a deep breath. She had to get a grip. She had to focus. Whether Reed was beginning to open up to the idea of fatherhood or not had nothing to do with her. And last night hadn't changed that. What they'd had was sex. Nothing more. She needed to keep that at the forefront of her mind. She needed to focus on why she was here. "I want to talk to Tiffany Maylor. I don't like the fact that we missed her last night. That party wasn't big enough for her to not hear the commotion you and Teddy Jr. stirred up."

"You think she was avoiding us."

"Maybe."

"I know one place we'll be sure to find her."

"Where?"

"Practice. The cheerleaders aren't allowed to miss practice. She'll be there. And while we're there, I can show you Texas Stadium." His eyes seemed to twinkle like emeralds, as if the prospect was the most exciting of treats.

Unfortunately, her mind skittered to a treat more delicious. A thought she pushed away. "Texas Stadium, huh? I'm supposed to jump up and down about that?"

"You're supposed to feel honored."

"Let me guess, you're a big Cowboys fan."

"Everyone around here is a big Cowboys fan. It's in the water."

"Like rivalries and fistfights and an overage of testosterone?"

He grinned at her teasing. "Like smart-ass humor and great sex."

She tried to ignore the surge in temperature that rippled over her skin. "So this Dallas Cowboys fixation. Was it part of your attraction to Honey?" She knew the image of Honey's perfect body in that uniform shouldn't still bother her. She knew Honey wasn't the one coming between her and Reed. But she couldn't ignore the sliver of jealousy that was still logged under her skin.

"I should find the number of personal questions you've been asking me lately disturbing."

"You don't?"

"I think I'm getting used to it. I think I might even be starting to like it."

The heat that enveloped her started to shimmer. This conversation was getting too hot for comfort. Too personal. Too intimate. She didn't want to imagine sex with Reed. Even more, she didn't want to imagine long, personal talks and intimate feelings. "You didn't answer the question. Tell me about your attraction to Honey." If that didn't cool her down and put things back into perspective, Josie didn't know what would.

Reed tilted his head. "I suppose the DCC thing was part of my attraction to Honey. At least at first. I mean, every red-blooded male dreams of dating a Dallas Cowboys Cheerleader. The reality is a little different."

"How so?" She let out a relieved breath. Better to discuss Honey than dwell on what she wanted there to be between them. Already, she could feel the sanity returning.

"Do you know how hard those women work? How many practices they have? And training camp? I was impressed with Honey's dedication, but truth was I didn't see her much during the time we were dating. Looking back now, I'm not sure I knew her all that well."

"And you were busy, too. With your mother."

"Yeah. She took a lot of my time. Always did, not that she could help it." Reed gave a wistful smile and shook his head. "So how about you? A Forty-niner fan?"

"Green Bay Packers. The real America's Team."

"Them's fightin' words, you know."

She gave him a smile. Light banter was easy. Effortless. And while her heart soared each time he confided something to her, she knew even the most trivial of details was pulling her bit by bit, word by word toward a cliff she couldn't let herself tumble over.

Troy spit out the nipple and made a face. She set the bottle on the bay windowsill and threw a burp cloth over her shoulder.

Reed held out a hand. "Let me."

She nodded. Once he draped the cloth over his own shoulder, she handed him the baby.

Reed positioned the baby and started patting his back like a pro.

The sight gave Josie a pain deep in her chest. The pain and longing shuddered deeper than any bubbly warmth sex talk could generate. "You're good at that, you know."

"I had a good teacher."

"You're a natural."

"Thanks. Coming from you, that means a lot." His eyes locked on hers, the irises the darkest and most pure shade of green she'd ever seen.

She knew she should look away. Call to check what time Esme would arrive, get ready to talk to Tiffany, focus her mind on other things. But she couldn't. At that moment, Reed was all she could think about. Everything she needed. The only thing she couldn't do without.

And she no longer had to worry about falling over that cliff. She already had.

Then a crack split the air, and the window exploded.

"GET DOWN!" REED CROUCHED on the floor, pulling Josie down with him. A gunshot. His heart slammed against his rib cage. Shards of glass crunched under his knees. Troy writhed stiffly against his shoulder and let out a loud squawk.

"The baby." Josie's voice trembled.

Oh God. Reed held the baby away from his shoulder.

He yowled. His fists flailed in the air. But despite the baby's alarm, he appeared to be unharmed. "He's okay. But we've got to get out of here."

"Do you have any weapons in this place? A shotgun? Anything?"

He shook his head. Right before he'd left Texas, he'd given the shotgun to their last ranch hand. A parting gift. And since Josie hadn't been able to bring her gun...

He'd never felt so helpless. He pointed to his cell phone, still on the coffee table, where he'd left it last night. "Call 911."

"See if this works to keep him quiet." Josie handed him the bottle. Leaving the baby in his hands, she crawled to the center of the living room on hands and knees.

As Troy clamped down on the nipple, Reed shifted to the side of the bay window and strained to hear any sounds from outside. From this angle, he could see part of the corral fence and the whitewashed barn beyond. No sign of movement. Not that he could see. Only the tweet of birds singing caught his ear.

He concentrated on slowing his breath, controlling

the adrenaline that buzzed through him, forcing his mind to think. He needed to protect Josie and the baby. He needed to find a way out of this.

Josie gave the dispatcher information in a low voice. She sounded so calm, so in control. Far from what he felt.

What if something happened to Josie? To the baby? What if he couldn't get them out of this mess?

That was it. Get them out, away from the ranch. He had to do whatever it took to keep them safe.

Cradling Troy in one arm, he used the other to crawl across the floor to where Josie sat. "The car is out in the drive. Do you think you can reach it?"

"Whoever's shooting… The gunfire came from the front of the house."

"I know. But if I distract him, draw his fire, do you think you can make it to the car? Get the baby out of here?"

"And what will happen to you?"

He hadn't thought that far ahead. "I'll figure something out."

"You think it's the guy from San Francisco? The one who hurt Missy?"

"I don't know. But whether it's him or someone else, it doesn't matter." He could kick himself for turning John Wise and Samantha Corely away. The man out there must have been waiting until they left, waiting until he and Josie and the baby were alone.

"Maybe it does matter."

"What do you mean?"

"If it is the same guy, we know he's after the baby, right? So our decoy should be the baby."

She was right. Not the baby, of course, but something that looked like the baby. "Where's the blue blanket?"

Josie pointed to the baby's bucket seat, sitting on the kitchen counter.

Reed handed Troy to her. First he had to find someplace for them to hide. Someplace they would be safe in case the shooter didn't fall for the bait.

He scanned the area within easy reach of the front door and the car beyond. While some houses had foyers and staircases and charming nooks and crannies, this house had none. The front door opened to a boxlike room. No concealed spots. No cover to protect Josie and the baby from gunfire. "Damn."

"What is it?"

"If I try to lead him away from the front door, and he doesn't fall for it, you're sitting ducks."

She shook her head. "I don't like you making yourself a target anyway. The police will be here soon. They're on their way."

"This isn't the city, Josie. It can take a while. Springton doesn't even have its own police department. They rely on the county sheriff."

Her face looked pale. Blood trickled from a cut in her scalp. Flying glass, no doubt.

No. As much as he'd like to believe the sheriff's office could have deputies here in time, he couldn't risk it. He had to do something.

A creak came from somewhere in the kitchen.

Reed glanced at Josie. Flattening his hand, palm down, he motioned for her to lie flat on the floor.

She hunkered down, sheltering the baby with her body.

Reed's pulse pounded in his ear. His breathing rasped in his throat. So much for deciding the best course of action. They were out of time. There was no good course of action left, if there ever had been one. All he could do now was stop that gunman.

And he had to do it any way he could.

His gaze fixed on the fireplace and the gnarled branches of mesquite he'd brought in with the idea of building a fire the first night they'd arrived in Dallas. Crawling to the hearth, he grasped one of the logs. It was green, all right. Heavy. Not much use for firewood, but for a club, it would do.

He stood and moved along the living-room wall toward the kitchen. He walked as lightly as he could, trying to keep his footfalls quiet, but his pulse thumped so loudly in his ears, he was unsure if he succeeded.

Reaching the corner, he flattened his back to the wall. From here he could see Josie's shadow under the couch, even though she was on the opposite side. No doubt, when the gunman came through the door, he'd see it, too. He'd know she was there. He'd know where to take aim and…

Another creak sounded from the kitchen, a step on a loose floorboard.

He gripped the branch and lifted it. He had to time this perfectly. If he swung too early, the guy could shoot him. If he swung too late, the guy would spot Josie's shadow. He'd have time to fire.

A shuffle came from just around the corner. The slightest of creaks vibrated across the board under Reed's foot. Dark hair, nearly black, crossed the threshold. Military short. Broad shoulders filled the space. He raised the barrel of his rifle.

Reed brought the branch down on the back of his

head. The force of his blow shuddered through his arm. A grunt escaped the man's lips. A rifle shot exploded in Reed's ears and ripped open the frame of the couch.

Chapter Fifteen

"No. No. No." The bellow filled Reed's ears, the sound coming from his own throat. He brought the branch down again and again until the man crumpled under it. Until the rifle fell useless to the floor.

He dropped the branch, now sticky with blood. The odor of blood filled his nostrils and clogged his throat. Blood and gunpowder.

The rifle.

Reed kicked the thing away from the man's still hands. It slid across the floor and hit the shattered couch. He stumbled across the floor after it, his feet unable to move fast enough. He stepped over the rifle and circled the pulverized fabric, wood and springs.

Josie curled and remained frozen on the floor, her body cupped around the baby, shielding him, protecting him, giving everything she had for him.

"God, Josie." He fell to his knees beside her. He swept ripped fabric off her and brushed slivers of wood from her hair. "You have to be okay. You have to…"

Underneath her, the baby squirmed. A scream tore from his throat.

She opened an eye and peered up at him through mussed strands of hair. "Where is he? Where is the gunman?"

"Are you okay?" He couldn't think about the crumpled shooter. Not now. All he could focus on was Josie and the baby. He couldn't breathe until he knew they were all right. "Answer me. Were you hit?"

"No. No. I'm okay." She shifted her shoulder back, revealing the squirming baby beneath her. "I think he's okay, too. I think he's just scared."

Reed braced Josie's shoulder, helping her up with shaking hands. She cuddled the baby to her chest. "What happened?"

"He's..." What he'd done to the gunman filtered into his mind. "I think I beat him to death."

Before he could make his body move, the door flew open and uniformed deputies burst into the room.

BY THE TIME THE DEPUTIES, EMS guys, crime-scene technician and Reed didn't know who else finally left the ranch, the day had stretched well into night. Hours had passed since their run-in with a man he learned was named Bobby Crabb, and yet he felt as if his insides were still vibrating from that shotgun blast and how close he had come to losing Josie and Troy.

He found Josie in the baby's room, watching him sleep in his football-themed playpen. At first he didn't say anything to let her know he was there. He just watched her. Taking in the tilt of her head and the gentle smile on her face. When she finally turned to look at him, he noticed tears sparkling in the corners of her eyes. "What's wrong?"

"Nothing."

"Right. There are a lot of ways you could have answered, but nothing is not one of them."

"Okay, I just…" She shook her head and looked back down at the baby.

He could guess how she was going to end her sentence. "Were thinking about how horrible it would be if something happened to him?"

She looked back up at Reed and bit her bottom lip. "What kind of a man tries to kill a baby?" Her voice shook.

With rage? With tears? He didn't know. But he could relate. "A hit man. That's what the sheriff's detective told me. His name is Bobby Crabb, and he's suspected of being a killer for hire."

"So who is he working for?"

"Once he recovers, I imagine the detective will ask him. And offer him a chance to escape the needle if he tells all." Reed had to admit he was relieved to find out he hadn't killed Crabb. The thought that he was capable of taking a human life had been sobering. Horrifying, really. Although he knew now he would truly do anything to protect Josie and that beautiful little boy. But also, if Crabb was alive and could be convinced to talk, the sheriff's office could arrest whoever hired him. And that might lead them to Honey. "As far as I'm concerned, they can't find out who hired him fast enough."

Josie nodded, but judging from her expression, her thoughts were far away.

"There's more news, too."

"Honey?"

He wished. Although not for the same reasons he had when he first learned she was missing. "Unfortunately, no. But remember Neil Kinney?"

"The guy whose car you bashed. How could I forget?"

He had to admit that move hasn't been very smart. No doubt a product of that extra testosterone in the water, as Josie had pointed out. But it was satisfying. "He was arrested."

"For what?"

"The detective wouldn't tell me. He just said he'd be in jail for a while, and if he had a guess, the bail was going to be set pretty high."

"Good. Do you think he's the one who hired this Crabb guy?"

"No. I don't think so. I just can't see Kinney hiring someone to take care of Honey. He'd want to do it himself." Even thinking about the creep made him angry. It was a relief not to have to think about him again. "Things are narrowing down. And if the detective can get Crabb to talk, it could be over soon."

He tore his eyes from the baby and glanced at Josie just in time to see a matched pair of tears slide down her cheeks. He reached out and wiped the glistening moisture away with his fingertips. "What is it?"

"Nothing."

"Come on. After all we've been through, you should be able to talk to me. I sure talked to you." About his failures. About his guilt. About feelings he'd kept under wraps his entire life. "I expected you to feel relieved by all this good news, not upset."

"I'm not upset. Not really."

"Right. Sure."

She pressed her lips together and swiped at her cheeks with the back of one hand. "It's just... It's personal."

"Do you want me to guess?"

"This doesn't have anything to do with you. Really. It's just something I want."

"A baby."

"Is that so bad?"

"Of course not. It does explain a few things, though."

"Like what?"

"Like why you were so angry with me when we first met. Not that you weren't right."

"I wasn't angry."

He looked at her out of the corner of his eye.

"Frustrated. I was frustrated."

He remembered her telling him some people would kill for the chance to have a baby like Troy. He must be slow. It had taken him until now to realize she was talking about herself. "So what's the hurry? You're young. You have plenty of time to have babies of your own."

"No, actually I don't."

He said nothing. He didn't know what to say. Or what the comment meant. But somehow he sensed if he just let her have a little time, she'd tell him.

"I can't have children of my own." Her voice was low, almost a whisper. "I had a growth when I was young. Just a kid, really. And anyway, a hysterectomy was the result."

He swallowed into a tight throat. He'd never really thought about having kids, not until little Troy showed up on his boat. He'd just assumed it was an option for him. Someday. Or not. Whatever he wanted. The thought that Josie, a woman who loved babies so much and was so good with them...the idea that she didn't have that choice...it wasn't right. "I'm sorry."

"I'm trying to adopt. I'm on a waiting list. A single

mother isn't the ideal candidate, but I'm working on changing my life so that I'm a better prospect."

"That's why you quit the police force?"

She nodded. "Being self-employed is a little risky financially. But if I can get my business off the ground, the flexibility of my schedule will work in my favor."

He pulled in a breath, a little easier this time. "Sounds like you have it all figured out."

"I thought I did."

"You don't anymore?"

"I didn't count on falling in love."

His breath hitched in his chest.

She nodded down at the baby splayed on the blanket covering the playpen's vinyl football field. "He's amazing, isn't he?"

Reed's breathing evened out, but this time his chest ached, empty. "Troy is amazing. He sure is." And even though he meant every word of it, he couldn't help wishing she'd said she'd fallen in love with him.

"I know I'm going to lose him. When this case is finished. Maybe very soon. But I keep telling myself he'll have a good life without me. He'll have parents who love him. Won't he?" She returned her gaze to his, and for a moment the look in her eyes took his breath away.

Reed slipped his arm around her shoulder, pulling her into his arms. She felt so soft, so real, so alive. He wanted that life. He wanted to soak it in and let it infuse his muscles, his bones. He wanted it to fuel his heart. "Esme says he looks like I did. And if he and his sister are mine, you can bet they'll have all the love they need. They'll have you."

Her warm breath and the brush of her lips sent chills

over his back and down his side. "Really?" She raised her head from his shoulder.

He kissed her, and she kissed him back, her lips accepting his, her tongue drawing him in. She tasted sweet and warm and addicting. She slipped her hands under the tail of his shirt. Her fingers fanned over his sides and back.

His skin came alive with shivers, alive with heat. He wanted her to touch all of him. He wanted to touch all of her. To meld with her. Become one.

He slid his hands up her sides, sweeping her shirt over her head. Then came bra, the jeans, the panties and she was naked. In a matter of seconds he was naked, too. He took her back into his arms and claimed her lips again, pressing the length of her body against his. Her skin felt so soft, so right—he couldn't get enough.

He ached to be inside her, but first he wanted to give her all she'd given him. He wanted her to feel as special as she deserved.

He scooped her into his arms and carried her to the bedroom.

A laugh sounded deep in her chest, sexy as hell. "This is awfully old-fashioned of you."

He had to agree. Old-fashioned verging on cliché. He gave her a smile. "I only wish I had candles or bubble bath or a bottle of really good wine. I want you to have all the trappings. Anything wrong with that?"

Her lips smoothed into a smile. "Nothing at all. Trappings are nice, but all I really need is you."

He laid her on the bed and stretched his body over hers. "You don't need anyone."

"You're wrong. I need you. I trust you. And I want you. Right now."

That was all he needed to hear. He skimmed his lips down her throat, over her collarbone and sucked her breasts. He kissed his way down the flat of her belly to her hips and burrowed between her legs. The first series of spasms that rocked her were sweet, the second even sweeter.

She threaded her fingers through his hair and guided him back up her body. "I need you right now. Inside me."

He kissed her and sank into her heat. Looping her legs around him, she urged him deeper. And at that moment he wanted to give her everything he could. Everything he was.

This was where he should be. This was where he belonged. It wasn't just the sex, but everything. How he felt. Who he wished to be. What the future before him held. And although he couldn't know who the twins' father was, for the first time he really wanted it to be him. More than anything, he wanted to make Josie's dream of a family come true.

And he was beginning to wonder if her dream had become his own.

THE PHONE RANG BEFORE dawn. Josie groaned. She didn't want to get out of bed. She wanted to stay there forever. Feeling. Letting go. Belonging to Reed and he to her. After their first encounter, she'd sworn she would never let him inside her, physically or emotionally. But last night she'd opened the door to both, and she never wanted to close that door again.

"Who's calling?" Reed lifted his head off the pillow, squinting at the darkness beyond the window blinds as if it were bright as blazing sun. "What time is it?"

"I don't know. The sun's just starting to come up, though."

"Who the hell would call before it's even dawn?"

Josie could think of only one explanation. "The sheriff's office?"

Reed groaned. "Like they weren't here late enough." He tossed the sheets back.

The scent of warm skin and lovemaking wafted over Josie. The leather and musk scent of Reed. The lighter scent of her own body. She took a deep breath.

She had an idea who might be on the phone, but as soon as she said it, last night's spell would be over. She and Reed would be plunged back into reality again. And she didn't want to give up the closeness they'd shared.

She knew he'd been honest with her about his feelings. She knew his feelings wouldn't shift like wind over the flat Texas landscape. She trusted him. Yet deep down she felt a niggle of doubt. The sense that once they left this bed, nothing would be the same. And she wanted to soak up every bit of this while she still could.

She put her hand on his shoulder before he could lever himself off the mattress. "Wait." She sat up, letting the sheets fall to her waist.

His gaze moved over her bare breasts, his eyes as hungry as they'd been last night. Forgetting the phone, he fondled a nipple with rough fingertips. "I'd say this is worth waiting for." He brought his lips to hers, the kiss deep and sweet and stirring.

This was what she wanted. What she couldn't get enough of. She skimmed her fingers down his chest and over his belly.

He was already erect. His length flexed in her fist.

Warmth pooled between her legs. Hot need. She moved her hand down to the base, up the underside of his shaft, then tickled the tip.

"Yes." Reed's hand toyed with one breast, then the other. He kissed her deeper, plunging into her mouth.

She was just about to lick her way down his body when the phone rang again.

Reed groaned under her lips.

Josie sat upright. The worry was back, and she couldn't put it off any longer. "It could be the detective. They might have found something. Or someone."

Giving her one last kiss, Reed thrust himself from the bed and located the phone. He punched the On button and held it to his ear. "Yeah?"

Josie watched his face. Even in the dim light and halfway across the room, she could see his open expression close down with each word the caller spoke. Her bad feeling spread. She tossed the covers off and started trying to locate her clothes.

"No comment." He punched the Off button.

"No comment?"

"Seems what happened last night is today's big news story."

"That was a reporter?"

"Yeah. And according to him, the judge is saying we have his baby. He's calling for us to do the decent thing and bring Troy to his ranch."

"But the baby might not be his." She'd always wished it, even when she was trying to play devil's advocate with Reed. But now Troy's parentage had taken on an even greater importance. She'd never been so close to getting everything she'd always wanted, everything she thought she'd never have.

"The baby isn't his. And he's not touching him."

The phone's ring sounded more shrill this time, more invasive. Reed turned it off.

"What if the detective finds something? What if he calls?"

"We can call him in a couple of hours. Check in. Right now we'd better get dressed. The first guy said he was with one of the cable news channels. I think they've decided it's a great story to break on their morning show."

"It's a national story?"

Reed nodded. "And they're sending over a camera crew."

By the time Josie got dressed and fed a now-awake Troy, not one but three camera crews had staked out the front yard. Every few minutes another one of their reporters would ring the doorbell. Every few minutes Reed and Josie would try once again to ignore the bedlam outside.

The chime echoed through the boxy little house once again. Someone pounded on the door with a fist. "Reed! *Por Dios.*"

Reed pushed back the kitchen chair and lurched to his feet. "Esme." He raced for the front door.

Josie could picture the gentle woman being pushed at and prodded by the story-hungry media outside. After Bobby Crabb's attack, Reed had told her they didn't need her to babysit, but had said nothing more for fear of worrying her. However, they'd forgotten Esme was still planning to stay with the baby this morning. If only they'd remembered, they could have called her and warned her away.

Voices came from the living room—Reed and other men. Heavy footsteps thundered across the floor. How many people were out there?

Esme scampered into the kitchen, her brown eyes wide with alarm. Reed and another man followed her. The man wore a tailored navy suit and pink tie, the outfit far more expensive than the suits of the newsmen outside.

Reed's expression was drawn, shuttered. A muscle along his jaw flexed.

Josie sat straight on her chair, trying her best not to telegraph her worry to the baby.

Reed nodded to her. "Josie, this is…"

"Steven Albright," the other man provided. "I represent Judge Teddy Wexler."

A cold chill skittered down Josie's spine. She held the baby to her shoulder and started patting his back. "I hope you don't think you're here to take Troy, because you're not going to get him."

"I'm afraid I have to disagree, Ms. Dionne. That child belongs to the judge. Ms. Dawson might have abandoned the child, but Judge Wexler certainly did not. As the baby's father, he has the right to assume custody under the law."

Josie's cheeks heated. She could feel Esme's shocked stare. Even though she had been worried something like this was coming, she felt plenty shocked herself. "Honey didn't abandon the baby. She trusted him to the care of Reed Tanner. The baby's real father."

Both Esme and the lawyer turned to look at Reed. The lawyer narrowed his eyes. "Real father? Do you have documentation to prove this?"

"We should soon." Josie knew she should probably

keep her mouth shut, let Reed take the lead. After all, Troy was potentially his child, not hers. And though Reed had told her he wanted the twins last night, a part of her was still uneasy about raising her expectations so high. She wasn't used to putting that much control over her own happiness into someone else's hands.

The lawyer turned to Reed. "Is this true?"

"Yes," he said in a strong voice. "I submitted samples for DNA testing. We should be getting the results soon. But I can tell you, I did have a relationship with his mother around the time he was conceived, and he shares many of my traits. So I think it's me who has the law on my side, and the judge who is going to have to prove he has any reason to suspect the twins are his."

"Twins?" Esme whispered, as if having trouble fitting any of it together in her mind.

Josie nodded. "A girl and a boy. We just talked to someone who located the little girl yesterday."

"Information you'll have to turn over to us," Albright said.

Reed let out a laugh. "Right. At the same time we give you this little guy." He didn't say it, but his inflection suggested it would be a cold day in hell before he let that happen.

Josie smiled at him. Her chest tightened, as if there wasn't room enough for her growing feelings.

As Reed led the lawyer out among the media, yet another ringing phone jangled her nerves. But this one was different. "My cell. Can you take him?"

Esme gathered the baby from her arms and took over the back-patting ritual, murmuring to him in Spanish.

Josie raced into the bedroom where she and Reed had

made love. Her cell was still on the beside table, where she'd left it. She flipped it open and held it to her ear. "J. R. Dionne."

"Josie? It's Simon. I have your results."

Chapter Sixteen

Reed knew there was something wrong as soon as he saw Josie's face.

She sat on a blanket on the floor watching Troy's awkward attempts to roll from tummy to back. But instead of the expression of wonder she usually projected while taking in his daring feats, red rimmed her eyes and furrows pinched her forehead.

He shot a questioning look at Esme.

The older woman gave a little shrug in response. "Miss Dionne received a phone call. She will not tell me what it was about."

Josie didn't look up from the baby. But Reed didn't have to catch her gaze to know what the phone call had been about.

An empty pain hollowed out just below his rib cage. "Esme? Would you mind heating up a bottle for Troy? Josie and I need to talk."

Esme stepped toward the baby, but Josie raised a hand, stopping her. "Could you leave him here while you warm the formula? Please?"

Esme glanced at Reed. He nodded, and she left the room.

Reed sat on the floor beside Josie. Stretching his legs straight out in front of him, he leaned back on shaky hands. Part of him didn't want to ask what he knew he had to. Part of him didn't want to know.

As if not knowing would change anything. As if he could choose what reality to believe.

He pulled in a deep breath. "It was the lab, wasn't it?"

Josie nodded. Her eyes glistened. "There was no match. The twins aren't yours."

A few days ago he'd wanted to hear that news more than anything. Now that he'd accepted the prospect of being a father, now that he'd embraced the dream of a family of his own, the news stung like a cruel and cheap joke.

"I just keep thinking about how empty my arms are going to feel without him in them. How dreary mornings are going to be without seeing his smile." Josie looked up from the baby. Tears coursed down her cheeks and dripped off her chin. "I don't want to give him up."

Reed's chest ached. He tried to breathe, but his lungs wouldn't fill with air. "I don't want to give him up, either."

Josie leaned toward him, and he wrapped her in his arms. Her shoulders shuddered. Hot tears dripped onto his shoulder and soaked into his shirt.

As painful as this moment was for him, he knew it was much worse for Josie. She had wanted babies her entire life, and she couldn't have them. She had endured adoption lists, waiting and disappointment. And this was her greatest disappointment of all.

A disappointment he had created.

He felt sick. He had drawn her into this mess. He had led her along. He'd even painted a vast fantasy of them as a family, a fantasy he'd wanted to believe in, but still a fantasy, however you cut it. He'd set her up to trust he'd be there for her, that he could give her everything she wanted, and all along he hadn't even been the one to father those children. He'd sold her on a fantasy he couldn't deliver.

He'd let her down.

He swallowed into an aching throat. He couldn't undo the damage he'd caused. All he could do now was try to lessen the pain she had to endure. Pain that was his fault. "I know how hard this is for you. I'm so sorry. If you want to go home, I can wrap things up here."

"You mean give Troy to the judge?"

Is that what he meant? He supposed it was. If the baby wasn't his, he had no other choice. Not unless Honey suddenly showed up. But if she hadn't shown up yet, he didn't see how she was going to magically appear now. "I can handle it. There's no reason you have to go through that."

"No reason? How about to be there for you?"

He didn't know what to say. The betrayal was so thick in her voice. He didn't know where it was coming from. "It's okay. There's no reason you have to put yourself through it. I don't need you to hold my hand. I can deal with it on my own."

"I know you can, but you don't have to. Whether the twins are yours or not, I'm here for you. Don't you believe that?"

He didn't know. All he could feel at the moment was a swirl of disappointment and hurt and confusion. But more than all of that, he felt the pain in Josie's voice. And he knew he had failed her. "I'm so sorry, Josie."

"For what?"

"I know you want a baby. More than anything. I'm sorry I couldn't give you that."

"Is that all you think I want?" Her eyes grew wider, glistening like sapphires. "Is that all you think we have?"

Was it? He didn't know. He'd had a picture in his mind. A picture that included four. To adjust to a picture of two was a big step. To adjust at all was a big step, and he'd been doing a lot of adjusting.

But all that aside, he knew why he was hesitating. It had taken a lot, but he finally saw what had haunted him all these years with his mother, through his time with Honey. And he could see what haunted him still. "I don't want to make things worse."

She shook her head, as if she wasn't following.

"I feel like I've failed you."

"Failed me? What are you talking about?"

He wasn't sure. It sounded so stupid when he said it out loud. Yet the feeling was there, deep as bone. "All my life, I couldn't give my mother what she needed. I couldn't be what she needed."

"And you think I need a baby."

"You said it yourself, Josie. And I could see it in your eyes every time you held Troy."

She looked down at the infant. The infant who wasn't his son.

The tender sadness in her eyes ripped his heart in two. "You can't deny it."

"I'm not denying anything. I always wanted a baby. The one thing I don't have control over. The one thing I can't get on my own." She brought her focus back to Reed. "But I can adopt. Eventually. I'm still on the list."

He nodded. The list. Her hope was amazing, especially while she still faced saying goodbye to Troy. But all he could focus on was how hurt she'd be if that list fell through, too. All he could care about was keeping her from being disappointed further. "It might take years for you to get the chance to adopt a child. You know that."

"Then I'll wait years. We'll wait years."

He couldn't speak. He didn't know what to say.

"We want a baby, don't we? I thought we were together on this. I thought you changed your mind. God, I'm so stupid."

"I did change my mind." He'd wanted a child. His child. And for Josie, he would even consider adopting. His concern wasn't about that. It wasn't about some future baby at all. "Years. That's a long time. Will I be enough until then? Just me? Alone? Or whenever you look at me, will you remember Troy and the twins I couldn't give you?"

"I won't."

"You can't promise that." And he wouldn't believe her if she did.

To her credit, she didn't answer, but she didn't have to. He could see her answer in the worried furrows on her forehead.

"I'll do a lot of things for you Josie, for the chance that we can be together. But I can't be a failure in your eyes. I can't be the guy who couldn't give you what you really want. I've lived that life, and I won't do it again."

JOSIE PULLED HER EMPTY suitcase from the closet and tossed it on top of the rumpled sheets where she and Reed had made love just hours ago. Less than a day had passed, and yet since then her entire world had changed.

She choked back a sob. She'd done more than enough crying in the past few days, more than she'd done the past many years combined. And yet it seemed she had plenty more tears to shed.

It seemed she could cry forever.

She threw a stack of jeans in the bottom of the suitcase, then piled in a few T-shirts and a garbage bag half full of dirty laundry. She hadn't brought a lot, and she didn't really care about making sure she brought it all home. None of those practical things felt important now.

All that mattered was Reed. All that mattered was Troy. And she couldn't take them. Neither of them belonged to her.

Reed would be returning to the city by the bay, but she doubted she would see him again. He'd made that decision for her and then wrapped it in the excuse that he was pushing her away for her own good.

What crap. She didn't feel he'd let her down. It was him who'd decided that. And she knew his decision was more about punishing himself, the way he'd done for his failure to fix his mother's life.

A failure that was never his either.

She tossed socks and underwear and a couple of bras into the suitcase and followed with her make up bag and toiletries. How ironic that she'd believed he was irresponsible when they first met. Reed was the most responsible man she'd ever known. He took responsibility for everything, even things which had nothing to do with him.

Like the fact that he hadn't fathered the twins.

Josie's chest ached. She couldn't think about what Troy's life would be like as the son of Judge Teddy Wexler. She couldn't picture him and his sister trying

to wring some affection from Portia or fighting the ob-
noxious Teddy Jr. for a chunk of the judge's inheritance. She could only hope Honey would show up.
Somehow. Somewhere. Or that Troy had absorbed
enough love in his first months of life to enable him to
get through it all.

She couldn't think of his future. She could only
hope and pray.

She stuffed a few last items in the side of the bag.
Shoes. Slippers she'd never worn. A digital camera
whose hard drive held precious photos of the baby she
had to leave behind. Her chest ached. Her arms felt cold.

She needed to hold him. Breathe in his sweet baby
scent one last time. Kiss his downy hair. See that killer
smile. She had no idea how she was going to walk out
that door. How she would climb aboard an airplane and
fly off to California, leaving him behind. Leaving Reed
behind. Leaving her dreams behind.

She couldn't do it.

His real parents would take custody. She couldn't
stop that. And Reed could push her away. But she didn't
have to give in. She couldn't.

She wouldn't.

She would be there if Reed had to hand Troy over to
the judge, whether Reed liked it or not. And she'd be
open to his call once they'd returned home. Maybe he'd
come around in time. Quit feeling like he'd failed her.
Quit blaming himself. Maybe they'd get another chance.
To get to know each other better. To date. Maybe even
to fall in love all over again.

Stranger things had happened.

She flopped the suitcase's flap closed and left the

room. If Reed wanted to withdraw, he could. But that didn't mean she had to. She would spend the last hours before the judge claimed Troy holding the little guy tight. Drinking him in. Soaking in enough memories to last until her name finally hit the top of that adoption list. Until she had a baby of her own.

She walked to the nursery door and slipped inside. Sunlight streamed through the blinds, leaving slats of light and shadow streaking the room…and falling across the empty playpen.

"WHERE IS HE?"

Reed looked up from the papers the judge's lawyer had given him. He still couldn't wrap his mind around the prospect of handing Troy over, and as he read the document, he searched for a way around giving the judge what he wanted. "Where's who?"

"The baby."

"Esme took him. She put him down for a nap."

"No, she didn't."

He frowned. He didn't know what Josie was getting at, but the panicked edge to her voice brought him to his feet. "Maybe she's out in the yard with him." Even to him, the idea sounded lame. What would she be doing out there? Treating him to a little sunburn? Showing him what peeling paint and overgrown weeds looked like?

"Her car." Josie made a beeline for the front door. As she pulled it open, shouts rose from the few reporters who had stuck it out for a comment from them after the judge's lawyer left. "It's not there."

Reed joined her at the door. Sure enough, the spot where Esme had parked, next to the barn, was empty.

A cramp assaulted the back of his neck. He grasped Josie's arm and pulled her back inside. "Maybe she took him for a drive."

"A drive? To where?"

He hadn't a clue. "Her phone. She has a cell phone. Her daughter insisted she get one. I'll call her."

He led Josie back into the kitchen. He was sure it was nothing. How could it be anything, really? Crabb was in the hospital. The judge was reaching through the legal system to get his hands on the baby, and there wasn't a chance they could stop him. Not if he came up with a DNA test that proved his paternity, anyway. So how could this be anything other than an innocent drive? "I'm sure it's nothing. Maybe she had to be somewhere and was worried we were too upset to handle the baby right now."

Josie's look made it clear what she thought of that idea. "You know her number?"

"She left it here." He located the slip of paper where Esme had jotted down her contact information. Grabbing the phone from its charger on the countertop, he punched in her cell number.

Esme answered on the sixth ring. *"Hola."*

"Esme. It's Reed. Do you have the baby with you?"

"Sí. I have him."

Reed nodded to Josie. "Why? Where are you heading?"

"I am doing what I should have done years ago. What your mother insisted I don't do. I'm doing what's right."

"You've lost me. I don't understand."

"You are not this baby's father."

So Esme had overheard his talk with Josie. He still didn't understand what his mother had to do with this.

And what in the world should Esme have done years ago? "It's true. I'm not. I just found out this morning."

"And so you should not have this baby. A baby belongs with his family."

A hitch caught in his gut. "Esme? What are you doing?"

"I will not lie. Not this time."

"Lie? Who's asking you to lie?"

"You lied to the lawyer. If I say nothing, I am lying, too."

She couldn't be doing what he thought. "Esme, where are you going?"

"I lied before. I let your mother convince me it was best. And I saw how wrong it was. For her. For you. And it was not good for my soul."

"Esme…"

"I will not listen. I will not lie. I am bringing this child to his real father, then he can get a test to prove the child is his. I will not let you stop me."

Chapter Seventeen

The Wexler Ranch looked the same as it had two days before. Horses grazed along white board fence. Autumn flowers flourished in elaborate beds surrounding the mansion. And the bright Texas sun sparkled on paned windows. But no matter how pretty and peaceful the ranch seemed, Josie could only see it for what it was underneath the facade. Another trophy built for the glory of Judge Teddy Wexler.

She gripped the armrest and willed Reed to drive faster down the winding, paved driveway. The thought of Troy trapped in this place a moment longer than he had to be made her sick. A baby wasn't a mere possession, like the house, like the ranch, like the items on the judge's credenza. Troy and his sister needed love, a home, a real family. God knew her family wasn't perfect. They were stubborn and meddling and just plain annoying at times. But she never doubted they loved her and truly wanted what was best. Even when Missy was setting her up on dates and her brother was refusing to give her the information she needed, she always knew they were there for her. She always knew that they loved her.

Something she doubted any of the Wexlers had a clue about.

But Esme did. "Why did Esme say she was doing this? I don't understand it."

"I don't, either. But I gather she thinks we are lying by keeping the baby away from the judge."

"The judge doesn't have any kind of paternity test proving he's the father." She knew it was wishful thinking on her part that he wasn't, but she couldn't help it. She was desperate. She was grasping at anything that would save Troy from the life she saw spread out in front of him.

"He doesn't have a positive test. Not that *I* can force the issue. I have a test that proves I have no claim at all."

No, now that they knew Reed wasn't the babies' father, he had no legal standing to force anything where the twins were concerned. And they couldn't even come close to proving the judge hired Bobby Crabb, at least not yet. "We need to find Honey."

"Or Jimmy."

"Yes." She'd forgotten about Jimmy. If he'd been telling the truth about sleeping with Honey during that same time frame, there might be another option. "He could sue for custody, too. That would likely mean Troy would go to a foster home, but at least he'd be away from the judge. Maybe that could buy us enough time to find Honey."

Reed nodded. "But first we have to get Troy back. I don't trust the system in the county. When the judge wants a certain outcome, he usually gets it." He swung around the last bend in the road and raced for the circle in front of the house.

Josie braced her hand on the dash. She didn't know

what was up with Esme, but she would lie, cheat and steal to keep that baby from being hurt. If she could stop it.

Esme's car sat near the grand home's front entrance. Reed slammed on the brakes. He and Josie bolted from the car almost as soon as it stopped. They took the front steps two at a time, and Josie slammed a fist into the doorbell.

The chime echoed through the foyer inside.

Louisa opened the door.

Reed pushed past her. "Where's Esme?"

The maid stepped back and covered her mouth with her hand.

Breezing past Louisa, Josie followed Reed through the foyer and into the parlor where they'd met with Portia Wexler. The former beauty queen stood next to the fireplace. Esme sat on one of the Queen Anne chairs, Troy in her lap. When the baby spotted them, he beamed an openmouthed smile.

It was all Josie could do to keep from snatching him from Esme's hands and dashing for the door.

Portia glanced from one to the other. "What are the two of you doing in my house?"

Reed spoke first. "I'm sorry for busting in like this, but the baby needs to come home with us."

"No," Esme said through gritted teeth.

Portia gave them a puzzled yet blank expression. "I don't understand what any of this is about. What is going on here?"

Reed focused on her. "The judge. Is he here?"

She stared at him as if the suggestion was absurd. "It's country-club day. He's golfing. What is all this about?"

"I bring you his child."

Portia faced Esme and looked down her nose at Troy.

She pursed her lips together. "Fine. Leave him here, and I'll tell the lawyers you've complied."

Over Josie's dead body. The law would have to force her to leave Troy in the custody of the judge. And after witnessing Portia's reaction to him, Josie had no doubts the woman had been lying through her teeth about her eagerness to fill this mausoleum with children's laughter. She probably wouldn't even want to hold him for fear of breaking a nail or getting spit-up on her designer jacket.

Josie had to get the baby out of here. "The man who attacked us yesterday was hired by the judge, Esme. He's a hit man named Bobby Crabb. He came after us in San Francisco. His job was to kill Honey, maybe kill the babies, as well. We can't leave Troy here."

As if performing on cue or just reacting to the stress in Josie's voice, Troy's smile faded and he began to fuss.

Portia scoffed. "Don't be ridiculous. My husband is a respected judge. Why would he do such a thing?"

"Because he doesn't want the babies as much as he says he does? Or maybe he does want them, but Honey got in the way. She wouldn't let him have custody. Whichever the answer, Honey Dawson has been missing for days now. And I can't help believing the judge is responsible."

"My God." Portia held a hand to her Botox-smoothed forehead and lowered herself into a chair. "Do you have proof of this? That my husband hired this person?"

Josie narrowed her eyes, not sure if Portia really was horrified or if it was all an act.

Reed took a step forward. "Not yet. But Bobby Crabb is in custody. And this is Texas. If he did something to

Honey, he'll get the death penalty…unless he rolls over on whoever hired him."

"And you think it's Teddy." Portia's voice was low, barely above a whisper.

Grudgingly, something inside Josie felt sorry for her, at least for the moment. It must be one thing to be married to a ruthless bastard and quite another to be the wife of a potential murderer. "You see why we can't leave Troy here, don't you, Portia? Not until we know the truth."

Portia nodded. "I won't let him have the baby. But the legal system will. He's the father, right?"

"He is." Esme's voice sounded flat and sure.

"You don't know that," said Josie. The baby might not be Reed's, but she didn't want to believe Troy was fathered by the judge until she saw the DNA comparison with her own eyes.

"I know."

How could the woman be so stubborn? So sure of something she couldn't truly know? Josie glanced at Reed. He knew Esme better than anyone. Couldn't he say something to convince her? Or if need be, couldn't they just grab Troy from the woman's arms and walk out the door? "Reed?"

"Esme, the judge might want to hurt Troy." Reed's voice rumbled low, gentle.

The older woman shook her head. Tears glistened in the corners of her dark eyes. "A father should know his child."

"No. Not if he doesn't care what's best for the child. If he wants to hurt the child, we can't let him have his way."

"The judge always gets his way," said Portia. "At least he always has. Until now."

Josie hadn't thought much of Portia, not since the first time they'd talked with her in this very room. The chance that there might be someone inside that cold shell after all was a shocker. Josie wasn't sure if she should believe it or not. "You'll let us take the baby?"

"I will not let you." Esme bolted up from her chair. "I will not sit by while a man is robbed of his children. This time I will not have this sin on my hands."

Troy's complaints grew in volume.

Josie shook her head. She knew Esme was upset. That was clear enough in the woman's trembling hands and shrill tone. But what she said...it didn't add up. It didn't seem rational. "*This time,* Esme? What do you mean, *this time?*"

The older woman's face grew ashen. She focused on Reed. "This has happened before."

Reed shook his head.

Josie looked from one to the other. "What am I missing here? What happened before?"

Reed eyed Esme. Lines dug into his brow and bracketed his eyes. "Something she said on the phone. Something about my mother." He shook his head again, as if refusing to believe whatever it was.

"Your mother." Esme shifted her weight from side to side. She jiggled the baby to comfort him, yet all the while, Josie could tell she was really speaking to Reed. "She wanted me to lie. To carry her secret. And I did. For years and years, I did."

Reed pressed his lips into a pale line.

Josie wanted to hold him, shield him, protect him from whatever it was Esme wanted to reveal. He had gone through so much with his mother. So much pain.

So much guilt. He didn't need Esme to pile on more. "Let's go. Let's just take Troy and get out of this place."

Reed heaved a deep breath. "What secret?"

"It was your father...." Esme's voice cracked. Tears caught in the creases in her cheeks and trickled to her chin.

"What about my father?"

"He didn't run off. Not like she said. He didn't leave you, Reed. He never knew you were born."

He didn't react. Not with a blink of his eyes, not with a tensing of his jaw. He just stared at Esme, still as a rock. "Why didn't she tell him?"

"She was afraid he would take you from her. She was afraid he would leave her with nothing."

"Like Honey." Josie breathed the words more than spoke them.

Esme nodded.

Tension hummed in Josie's ears. She didn't want Esme to go on. She wanted to grab Reed and rush him out before...what? Before Esme could tell him the truth?

"Who?" Reed asked.

Esme paused. She glanced at Portia.

The aging beauty queen glared at Reed. Her lips were pulled back slightly from her teeth, and her shoulders hunched forward.

"Your father is the judge, Reed," said Esme. "So you see, I helped rob him of one child already. I can't live with stealing another."

REED'S MIND WENT NUMB. He wouldn't believe it. He couldn't. "That's ridiculous, Esme. I don't know why you're saying this, but the judge is not my father."

"He is."

He shook his head. Visions of the judge's credenza rippled through his memory. The photo of the football team. The resentment and rivalry between him and Teddy Jr. The way he used to envy the white board fence, the stories of the football field in the backyard, the thought of a father's pride at his son's accomplishments.

The whole thing was too ironic to be true.

Portia's laugh tinkled through the room, brittle as shards of glass. "First these twins, now Reed Tanner? No. I'm sorry. It's not going to happen."

"It is the truth." Esme stomped a foot on the thick carpet.

"How do you know?" Portia spat the question. "Do you have a paternity test? Or are you just looking to siphon off a little easy money?"

"Katie confided in me. She begged me to keep her secret."

"Katie Tanner was crazy. Everyone knows that. And anyone with half a brain wouldn't believe a word from that woman's mouth."

Reed could feel Josie's concerned gaze fall on him. He wanted to tell her he was okay. The whole idea that the judge was his father was ridiculous. And although Portia's cruel words cut into him, he couldn't pretend they weren't true.

Esme raised her chin. "I have proof."

"What proof?" Portia rested her fists on her hips.

"A photograph of the two of them together. Back before Reed was born."

Portia wiped away the claim with a wave of her hand. "So Teddy likes to noodle around. So what? That's not proof. That's not even a surprise."

"How do you think Katie got that ranch?"

"I suppose you are trying to say he bought it for her."

"I have the papers to prove it."

Portia shook her head. "That's still not proof."

"They can take a DNA test," Josie said. She watched Reed, forehead furrowed over worried eyes. "If you want to know."

Did he? Maybe when he was a teenager, when he was sure all the world had a life better than he did, especially Teddy Wexler, Jr. But now, as an adult? No. He couldn't think of anything he wanted to know less than that.

Portia whirled on a spiked heel and strode across the room.

Reed let out a breath. He didn't feel sorry for Portia anymore. Nor did he pity his mother. He was just tired of the whole thing. The secrets. The lies. The rivalries. It didn't matter to him if the judge was his father or not. But Troy? His whole life was ahead of him. At least if Reed was the judge's son, that would mean Troy was not. And while Reed couldn't do much if the baby's DNA matched the judge's, he wasn't going to allow the baby to be part of this world even for as long as a DNA test would take to complete. Not if he could help it. "I'm sorry you've had that on your conscience all these years, Esme."

"No. I am sorry. I stole from you just as much as Katie did. You could have had better. A father who would have been proud of you. Money. Not the hard life you had. You deserved more. You still do." She glanced around at the crown moldings and gold-framed land-scapes on the wall. "I will never forgive myself for keeping all this from you."

Reed glanced around at the opulent house. Esme had it all wrong. He'd never wanted this. Not really. This was the world his mother wanted, not him. And despite Esme's insistence that he was the judge's son, the more Reed thought about it, the more he doubted it.

His mother wanted riches. She wanted everything Reed could have given her *if* he was indeed the judge's son. That was why he'd always felt he'd failed her. He had. His genetics had. Katie Tanner might have tried to get pregnant with the judge's baby, or she might have just indulged in the fantasy. Whichever the answer, Reed was pretty sure he wasn't the judge's son. Because if he was, his mother wouldn't have kept it a secret. Not for a second. Not when by telling her secret, she could have gotten a piece of the Wexler pie.

No wonder he'd always sensed he wasn't enough for her. He wasn't. Only by being Teddy Wexler's son could he have possibly been enough. And knowing all he now did about the judge, that was a failure he was all too happy to own.

If only it didn't mean there was still a chance Teddy Wexler could claim Troy.

He turned away from the nanny who had raised him and met Josie's beautiful eyes. Eyes that beamed love and support and fierce independence. Eyes that could see what was important in life and had recognized something worthwhile in him. "Let's get out of here. The three of us."

Josie nodded. Holding out her arms for Troy, she stepped toward Esme.

"No one is going anywhere." Portia's voice echoed from behind him, no longer the weak whisper or the

Chapter Eighteen

Reed pulled his gaze from the gun in Portia's hand and focused on her face. She really did look so much like his mother. Beautiful in a brittle way. Fragile as a porcelain doll. He had to wonder what other similarities they shared. Something in his mother had shattered long ago. Was he now watching Portia Wexler shatter? Or had she done so long before this? "You hired Bobby Crabb, didn't you, Portia?"

Josie stepped in front of Esme, shielding the baby with her body.

Portia pursed her lips. The pistol shook in her fist.

It had been a guess. A hunch. But judging from her silence, it was a good one. "You didn't hire him to kill only Honey, did you? You wanted him to make the twins go away, too."

"I was Miss Texas. I could have had any man. Do you know what I gave up to have this life?"

Reed took a step toward her. If he could distract her, manage to get close enough, maybe he could take the gun away. Maybe he could stop her from hurting anyone. "Crabb is going to talk. He's going to give the police your name. If you turn yourself in, things won't be so bad. No one has been killed. The D.A. will go easy."

"Do you know how humiliating it is to have your husband all over town with one young thing or another? And then to have him get one pregnant? With twins?"

Reed took another step. Then another. His whole body hummed. He could feel Josie behind him. Standing strong between the baby and Portia. Watching him. He could see every detail of the gun in Portia's hand. A weapon that could steal all he'd been searching for in the space of a heartbeat, all Josie had given him, all he'd discovered in himself.

"When he told me I had to raise the brats, raise them so they could take a slice of my money…" Portia shook her head. "Too much. Too much. And now you want a piece of what's mine, too?"

"I don't want a piece of anything, Portia."

"Everyone wants a piece. You want a piece. The babies…they want two pieces. And if I don't shut my mouth and do what Teddy says, I don't get any piece at all."

"So that's why you hired Crabb to kill Troy and his sister." Reed inched forward. He wanted her to look at him, focus on him. Turn the gun on him and forget about Troy and Josie and Esme.

Portia didn't waver. "Crabb wasn't as good as he bragged he was. But that's not surprising for these parts, is it? I mean, none of the men around here are as good as they like to think. Not the ones I've known. Only a woman can really do what needs to be done."

Reed's pulse thundered in his ears. He took another

step. There was too much carpet left between them. Too much space. "You don't want to do this, Portia."

"Oh, I do." Her arm moved.

Reed leaped. His body slammed into Portia, and the gun exploded in his ears.

JOSIE'S TEARS STARTED flowing the moment Reed's eyes fluttered open.

He lay propped in the hospital bed, an IV dripping who knew what into his bloodstream. She expected him to look pale and weak, as Missy had after the attack. Even though the bullet Portia fired hadn't hit any organs, it had left a gash in his side that had cost him a lot of blood and required many stitches to close. But he appeared as strong and gorgeous as ever. In fact, he looked as if he could take on the world.

"What are you crying about? I'm the one who was shot."

She smiled through her tears. Leave it to him to tease her first thing. Give him another few minutes and he'd no doubt be making suggestive comments. "I thought you were dead."

"Me, too." He tried to sit up. Flinching with pain, he relaxed back into the bed. "Is everyone okay? Troy?"

"He's fine. Esme, too. And Portia is in custody. You saved us, you know. You saved all our lives."

"I done good, didn't I?"

Her heart squeezed deep in her chest. "You sure did."

"You know what my secret was?"

"What?"

"I wasn't worried about dying. I was far more worried about losing you." He lifted his hand from the bed.

She took it in hers, their fingers joining, careful to avoid the IV needle. Touching him felt so right. As it had from the beginning. Only, now she no longer fought her feelings. Now her feelings had long since won.

He looked down at their entwined fingers. "Remember when I said I didn't need you to hold my hand?"

"Yeah."

"I was wrong. I do. I need that more than anything."

The room wavered, watery through her tears. "Good. Because I'm going to do it whether you want me to or not."

He chuckled, a beautiful sound. "That's the Josie I know."

She leaned over him. Her hair swung down, brushing his cheeks, forming a curtain around their faces. She brushed his lips with hers. The touch was light, gentle, but it carried with it a wallop of feeling.

"I'm not broken, you know. At least my lips aren't."

She laughed and stood straight. "We'll see what the doctor says before we let loose." A memory flashed through her mind. "I almost forgot. I talked to that child advocate from Georgia, Samantha Corely. She's Honey's childhood friend, the one whose name you were trying to remember. And she and the police chief, John Wise, found Honey."

"Is she…"

"She's in rough shape, but she's alive. And Sam said she was going to be okay."

"Thank God."

Her sentiments exactly. "You know, after all I've learned about Honey, I feel like I know her better than most people. I'm looking forward to actually meeting her."

"You'll like her. She's sweet. And she likes children almost as much as you do."

Josie couldn't help but smile at that. She'd known since she'd first laid eyes on Troy that he had a mother who loved him. She just hoped Honey was able to raise the twins without interference. "Sam said Honey is planning to fight the judge for the babies' custody."

"Good. If I can get out of this place, maybe we can do something to help." As if to prove his point, he levered himself up on his elbows, grimacing with the effort.

"You can start helping Honey by lying back in bed and resting." She splayed a hand on the center of his chest and gently pressed him back into the bed. "Keep that up and you'll never get out of here."

"Did Sam tell you anything else? How is the baby girl?"

"She's with Honey. She sounds adorable. Sam said her name is Emmie."

A grin spread over his lips. "Troy and Emmie."

"Does that mean something?"

"Troy Aikman and Emmitt Smith. Really, Josie. If we're going to be spending serious time together once we get back to San Francisco, you're going to have to bone up on your Dallas Cowboys football trivia."

The thought of spending serious time together made her heart beat a little faster. She arched her eyebrows and returned his cocky grin. "Really? You have a lot more studying to do than I do."

"How's that?"

"The Packers have a longer history. More trivia."

"I thought the answer to every Green Bay Packer question was Brett Favre."

"Oh, you have a lot to learn."

"Well, I can't wait for you to teach me."

Josie's chest grew tight, but not from fear or stress or mistrust. This time she was filled with so much happiness, she didn't have room inside to accommodate it all.

There were only a couple more things hanging on her mind. "Why do you think Esme believed the judge was your father? A picture?"

"That, and she might be right about him buying my mother the ranch. From all appearances, they were an item. He might have wanted to have her close by. More convenient that way. Who knows?"

"Still, it doesn't seem like much to go by."

"I can't pretend to know everything Esme was thinking, but I know my mother, and I'm sure she told a convincing story."

Josie still didn't understand. "Why would your mother lie?"

He shrugged a shoulder, the movement making him flinch in pain "It would have made her feel important. I'm sure she wished I was the judge's son. It would have given me a piece of the Wexler fortune and prestige."

She hated to bring the last thing up, but she knew she had to. "Speaking of the judge…"

The grin fell from Reed's lips. "What about him?"

"Are you going to have a test done?"

"No."

"You don't even want to know?"

"He's not my father. I wish he was, because that would mean he has no claim on Troy and Emmie, but he's not."

She frowned. He seemed so sure. "How do you know?"

"It's not the sort of thing my mother would have kept

secret. Remember, she was a lot like Portia." He squeezed her fingers in his. "If there's one thing I've learned through all of this, it's that genetics isn't the important thing when it comes to family."

"What's the important thing?"

"Love. I love you, Josie Renata Dionne."

A warm tingle spread over Josie's skin and centered in her chest. Before she met Reed, she'd almost given up on love. It seemed too difficult. Too uncontrollable. Impossible to trust. She'd decided to get used to doing without a romance, to skip that step and move right to having a baby.

Maybe she was missing out. Maybe her brother had been right.

Now she needed to return Troy to his mother. But she couldn't be too sad. She'd had her faith in love restored. And maybe down the road she would get everything on her list. Everything she truly wanted. "I love you, too, Reed Tanner."

He brought her hand to his lips and kissed each finger. "I know all of this has happened way too fast. We haven't known each other long, and you haven't always thought that much of me."

She tilted her head to the side. "Only because I didn't know you."

"Okay, then promise me this. When we go back to San Francisco, let's spend time getting to know each other. A lot of time. Every day."

"That's a deal." Josie's heart danced. She felt dizzy, giddy and downright drunk. She leaned her head down and claimed his lips in a kiss.

And she didn't hold back.

Epilogue

Reed had underestimated how relieved he would be to see Honey alive and well, though he would have preferred their reunion had happened somewhere else.

He engulfed her in a hug, trying to ignore the tension buzzing in the air around them. "I'm so glad you're okay."

Honey nodded. Pulling back from the hug, she gave him a little smile. "Thank you for taking care of Troy. I knew I could count on you to keep him safe."

Funny—she'd known it when he hadn't known it himself. "I had help. Someone I want you to meet."

He nodded to John Wise and Sam Corely, who had walked into the law-office lobby behind Honey. A skinny man in a suit, who Reed presumed was Honey's lawyer, tagged along behind.

"Nice to see you, Tanner," Wise said. He offered his hand.

Reed gripped his hand firmly and shook. "I'm glad circumstances are a little better than the last time we met."

Wise shifted a nervous glance at the conference-room door. "Let's hope circumstances keep improving."

So the cop...check that...*police chief* of Honey's

hometown, Butterville, Georgia, was as apprehensive about this meeting as he was. Next to him, Honey fidgeted, twining her fingers together and shifting her feet on the marble floor. Behind her, Sam rubbed her hand over the pink bundle she held to her shoulder.

Reed grinned despite the tension. "Is this…"

Honey and Sam beamed in tandem. Honey gestured to the baby. "Reed, meet my daughter, Emmie."

He stepped around Samantha and peered over her shoulder. "Hello, Emmie."

The little face was delicate and angelic, yet she had a strength about her that made Reed smile. Her mouth stretched into a giant yawn.

In the hospital he'd gotten a chance to talk to Sam and John on the phone, and they'd told him Emmie and Honey had been through a lot. He couldn't help but wonder what challenges they'd faced. And what further challenges all of them would have to deal with once they walked through that conference-room door.

"You have Troy?" Honey asked.

Reed motioned to the conference room. "He's inside, along with that special person I want you to meet."

He led Honey, Sam, John and the lawyer into the conference room.

The judge sat at one side of the huge conference table, his lawyers flanking him. Glaring at Honey, he crossed his arms over his chest.

Honey looked straight ahead.

Smart woman. Reed focused on the far side of the room.

Josie sat in a high-backed conference chair. A clean diaper thrown over one shoulder, she held Troy against her heart and patted his back. When she spotted the group coming toward her, she broke into a tense smile.

Honey raced for Josie and Troy and covered her baby boy's face in kisses.

Reed introduced them. After much oohing and aahing, and Honey's tears over being reunited with Troy, Reed slipped an arm around Josie. "If you want to thank someone for taking care of Troy and keeping him safe, Honey, this is who you need to talk to. I couldn't have done it without her—found out who was trying to hurt him *or* taken care of a baby. Hell, I didn't even know I had it in me."

"Thank you." Honey gave Josie a hug. "He's a good guy."

"I know." Josie nodded. She nodded toward the baby, now lifting his head shakily from her shoulder and looking at all the people in the room with googly eyes. "Do you want to hold him?"

Honey patted her arm. "You can for now. I can tell you want to. It's okay."

Josie mouthed a thank-you, tears pooling in her eyes.

Reed shifted his feet on the low carpet. It was going to be a tough day. No matter how this meeting turned out, Josie and he would have to say goodbye to Troy. The best they could hope for was that he'd go home with Honey for good, with no more threat from the judge.

A prospect that didn't seem likely.

"Ticktock. Ticktock," the judge called out.

The judge's lawyer, who had come to Reed's ranch what seemed like forever ago among the television news cameras, checked his watch and stood. "If everyone will take a seat, we need to get started."

They shuffled into seats. Honey placed her baby bag in the chair beside her.

"As you all know," the lawyer droned, "we're here to see if we can reach an agreement about the custody of the children known as Troy James Dawson and Emmie Samantha Dawson. My client has been very patient in this matter, but he is eager to have contact with his twins."

A knock sounded on the door. It opened, and Jimmy stepped inside. "Sorry to interrupt, but I—"

"What are you doing here?" the judge asked in a loud voice.

"Jimmy!" Honey sprang from her seat and catapulted across the room. Even from this angle, Reed could see tears streaming down her cheeks. She hugged Jimmy and gave him a big smack on the lips.

The judge scoffed. "This is outrageous. We're in the middle of a meeting here. Sit down."

If Honey noticed the judge, she didn't react. When the kiss ended, she peered into Jimmy's eyes. "Oh, Jimmy. All those nights when I thought I was a goner, I kept seeing your face. Of all the people I wished I could see one last time before I died, I wanted to see you the most. I have something I need to tell you."

Jimmy lifted a hand. He wiped the tears from her cheek with gentle fingers, then cupped her face as if it was the most precious thing in the world. "What is it, sweetheart?"

"I love you, Jimmy."

He looked at her as if he was afraid to believe her words.

"It's true. I know I always said you were my friend, my buddy. But you're more than that. I just didn't see it. I was so stupid."

"You love me?"

"With all my heart. If you'll have me."

"Are you kidding? I've wanted you since the first time I saw you."

"Blah, blah, blah," the judge boomed. "All these hearts and flowers are real nice, but you're wasting my lawyers' time. Do you have any idea how much they charge? For God's sake, sit down."

Honey wrinkled her nose at the judge. Taking Jimmy's hand, she led him to the chair next to hers. She removed the baby bag and set it on the floor.

Jimmy looked over at Reed and gave him a civil nod.

Reed returned the gesture. So miracles did happen.

"Now, where were we?" the lawyer said.

"We were getting my kids," the judge snapped.

Reed leaned back in his chair. A headache pounded at the back of his neck. His side and chest ached, and he knew the pain wasn't just from his still-healing injury. He didn't want to listen to one word. Didn't want to sit here one more second. He thrust his chair back from the table and stood.

The judge made a growling sound low in his chest. "What do you think you're doing, Tanner?"

Reed leveled a look at the judge. "The baby needs changing. Do you think you're up to it, Judge?"

A muscle twitched in the judge's cheek.

"Didn't think so."

Honey stood. "I can—"

Reed held up a hand. "It's okay. I'll get it. One last time?" He'd just learned how to perform the procedure and wasn't ready to give up his new skill yet.

Honey gave him an understanding smile. "Knock yourself out."

He held out his hands, and Josie peeled Troy off her shoulder. Shutting out the twinge from his still-healing bullet wound, he carried the baby to a small sofa behind Honey and Jimmy. Josie followed with the baby bag she'd packed.

Doing his best to ignore the droning voice of the judge's lawyer, Reed worked as a team with Josie. She laid down the changing pad, and he placed the baby on top. He took off the dirty diaper while she unfolded a clean one and handed him the package of wipes. Strange. Just a short time ago, he would have walked across coals to avoid changing a baby's diaper. Now he was going to miss it. He wiped Troy's little bottom for the last time.

"Oh my God." Jimmy pushed back his chair and sprang to his feet. He stepped over to the sofa where Reed and Josie were changing Troy and knelt next to the baby.

Honey followed. "What is it?"

"For the love of…" The judge exploded. "What's going on around here? Can't we get through a simple meeting?"

Jimmy extended a finger and pointed to a small darkened patch on the baby's left hip. He looked up at Honey and stuttered, as if he couldn't find the words he wanted to say.

Sam Corely and John Wise crowded around them. Sam spoke first, cradling Emmie close. "It's a birthmark. Emmie has one like that, too. Right in the same spot."

Jimmy looked up at Honey with watery eyes. "And I do, too. Just like my father."

For a moment the air seemed to leave the room. Reed struggled to pull in a breath, then another. Suddenly his shocked mind cleared. "Jimmy is the twins' father."

Josie grinned at him and nodded.

"Sorry, Judge," John called out, grinning broadly. "It looks like you're going to have to find some other babies to win your awards for you."

The judge brought a fist down hard on the table. "I want a paternity test."

"And you'll get one," Honey said, but her smirk testified to how little the results worried her.

Josie slipped the clean diaper under Troy, and Reed covered him up and fastened the tapes before they had a waterworks show all over the fancy law firm's conference room.

Honey gathered her son from the bench and plunked him into Jimmy's arms, then took Emmie from Sam. The babies cooed in tandem as their mother and father cuddled them close and the four of them became a family.

As everyone filed from the conference room, Reed and Josie stayed behind. Reed reached a hand up and ruffled Josie's hair.

She gave him a tear-soaked smile. "He'll have a good family, won't he?"

Reed nodded. "I think he will."

"I'm glad."

"I'm going to have to come back to Dallas now and again. At least until the ranch sells."

"Really?"

"I don't know if I've mentioned this to you, but I sure hate to travel alone."

She smiled. "Then I'll make sure you don't have to."

"You think Honey and Jimmy will let the twins call me Uncle Reed?"

"I imagine they'll let them call you anything you want."

"Aunt Josie?"

Her smile widened, and the tears flowed harder, all at the same time.

"Don't be sad."

"I'm not sad. I'm happy that the judge isn't any part of this. That the twins will grow up with parents who really love them."

"That's all?"

"I'll miss Troy, of course. But like you said, we'll visit."

"And maybe, down the road, we'll find a way to get that baby you want."

Josie nodded.

"You still want that baby, don't you?"

"Of course. But there's something I learned throughout all this, too."

"What's that?"

"A baby isn't the only thing I want." She leaned forward and gave him a kiss so deep and hot he felt it blaze all the way to his groin. Pulling back, she gave him a teasing smile.

"Not the only thing, huh? Getting greedy?" That was sure as hell how he felt at the moment.

"Greedy? Maybe. It's just that with you, all things seem possible."

He leaned in to kiss her again. "That's what I like to hear."

* * * * *

To hear Emmie's story leading up to her reunion with Honey, be sure to pick up Rita Herron's PEEK-A-BOO PROTECTOR, on sale now from Harlequin Intrigue!

We'll be spotlighting a different series every month throughout 2009 to celebrate our 60th anniversary.

Look for Silhouette® Nocturne™ in October!

Travel through time to experience tales that reach the boundaries of life and death. Bestselling authors Lindsay McKenna, Cindy Dees, P.C. Cast and Merline Lovelace join together in a brand-new, four-book Time Raiders miniseries.

TIME RAIDERS

August—*The Seeker*
by *USA TODAY* bestselling author Lindsay McKenna

September—*The Slayer* by Cindy Dees

October—*The Avenger*
by *New York Times* bestselling author and
coauthor of the House of Night novels P.C. Cast

November—*The Protector*
by *USA TODAY* bestselling author Merline Lovelace

Available wherever books are sold.

nocturne™

New York Times bestselling author
and co-author of the House of Night novels

P.C. CAST

makes her stellar debut
in Silhouette® Nocturne™

THE AVENGER

Available October wherever books are sold.

REQUEST YOUR FREE BOOKS!

2 FREE NOVELS PLUS 2 FREE GIFTS!

HARLEQUIN®

INTRIGUE®

Breathtaking Romantic Suspense

YES! Please send me 2 FREE Harlequin Intrigue® novels and my 2 FREE gifts (gifts are worth about $10). After receiving them, if I don't wish to receive any more books, I can return the shipping statement marked "cancel." If I don't cancel, I will receive 6 brand-new novels every month and be billed just $4.24 per book in the U.S. or $4.99 per book in Canada. That's a savings of close to 15% off the cover price! It's quite a bargain! Shipping and handling is just 50¢ per book.* I understand that accepting the 2 free books and gifts places me under no obligation to buy anything. I can always return a shipment and cancel at any time. Even if I never buy another book from Harlequin, the two free books and gifts are mine to keep forever.

182 HDN EYTR   382 HDN EYT3

Name _____ (PLEASE PRINT)

Address _____ Apt. #

City _____ State/Prov. _____ Zip/Postal Code

Signature (if under 18, a parent or guardian must sign)

Mail to the Harlequin Reader Service:
IN U.S.A.: P.O. Box 1867, Buffalo, NY 14240-1867
IN CANADA: P.O. Box 609, Fort Erie, Ontario L2A 5X3

Not valid to current subscribers of Harlequin Intrigue books.

Are you a current subscriber of Harlequin Intrigue books and want to receive the larger-print edition? Call 1-800-873-8635 today!

* Terms and prices subject to change without notice. Prices do not include applicable taxes. Sales tax applicable in N.Y. Canadian residents will be charged applicable provincial taxes and GST. Offer not valid in Quebec. This offer is limited to one order per household. All orders subject to approval. Credit or debit balances in a customer's account(s) may be offset by any other outstanding balance owed by or to the customer. Please allow 4 to 6 weeks for delivery. Offer available while quantities last.

Your Privacy: Harlequin is committed to protecting your privacy. Our Privacy Policy is available online at www.eHarlequin.com or upon request from the Reader Service. From time to time we make our lists of customers available to reputable third parties who may have a product or service of interest to you. If you would prefer we not share your name and address, please check here. ☐

HI09R

You're invited to join our Tell Harlequin Reader Panel!

By joining our new reader panel you will:

- Receive Harlequin® books—they are FREE and yours to keep with no obligation to purchase anything!
- Participate in fun online surveys
- Exchange opinions and ideas with women just like you
- Have a say in our new book ideas and help us publish the best in women's fiction

In addition, you will have a chance to win great prizes and receive special gifts!
See Web site for details. Some conditions apply.
Space is limited.

To join, visit us at
www.TellHarlequin.com.

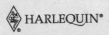
INTRIGUE®

COMING NEXT MONTH
Available October 13, 2009

#1161 ONE HOT FORTY-FIVE by B.J. Daniels
Whitehorse, Montana: The Corbetts
He's a practicing lawyer with a cowboy streak, and his wild side has been on hold…until he senses the danger that threatens the one woman who sees his true self.

#1162 THE SHARPSHOOTER'S SECRET SON
by Mallory Kane
Black Hills Brotherhood
The air force taught him honor and responsibility, but it was his ex-wife who taught him to love. When she's kidnapped by a group of terrorists trying to bait him, he makes it his mission to rescue her and rekindle the past they once shared.

#1163 CHRISTMAS GUARDIAN by Delores Fossen
Texas Paternity
Despite his dark past, the millionaire security agent falls for the helpless infant left on his doorstep. But when the baby's mother returns—with killers following close behind—he vows to protect his son and the woman who has captured his heart.

#1164 INTERNAL AFFAIRS by Jessica Andersen
Bear Claw Creek Crime Lab
She is shocked when her ex-lover, an internal affairs investigator, returns from the dead. Injured and unable to remember who he is, all he knows is there is an urgent mission he must complete.

#1165 COLORADO ABDUCTION by Cassie Miles
Christmas at the Carlisles
When her ranch becomes a target for sabotage just weeks before Christmas, the FBI send one of their most domineering and stubborn agents to ferret out the truth. And as the attacks escalate, so does the passion.

#1166 AGENT DADDY by Alice Sharpe
To take care of his orphaned niece and nephew, the FBI agent resigns from his dangerous job. But when his past follows him to the ranch, he fights for the new life—and love—he's just found.

HICNMBPA0909